W9-BYC-516

He was down there on the beach, waiting for her, in the middle of a raging storm— quixotic, impossible, in love. . . .

Lily was drenched in less than a minute as she hurried down the steps of the cottage. She lost her soaked slippers as she dashed across the sand to him. Nothing existed in the world except darkness and lightning and thunder.

Then she saw him coming to meet her.

"Go home!" she shouted, above the surf and the storm. "Don't you have any sense at—"

His mouth was crushing hers, hot, open, fierce.

She groaned as she collapsed against him. "No, Andrew, this isn't—"

"Yes, it is." He pulled her soaked robe off and let it fall to the sand. "Don't lie to yourself, love. This is why you're here." His hands wrapped her waist, pulling her tightly against him. "Lord, you feel so good."

She moved helplessly toward him. Sweet heaven, he was right, this was why she was here. All the rest was lies. . . .

WHAT ARE *LOVESWEPT* ROMANCES?

They are stories of true romance and touching emotion. We believe those two very important ingredients are constants in our highly sensual and very believable stories in the *LOVESWEPT* line. Our goal is to give you, the reader, stories of consistently high quality that may sometimes make you laugh, sometimes make you cry, but are always fresh and creative and contain many delightful surprises within their pages.

Most romance fans read an enormous number of books. Those they truly love, they keep. Others may be traded with friends and soon forgotten. We hope that each *LOVESWEPT* romance will be a treasure—a "keeper." We will always try to publish

LOVE STORIES YOU'LL NEVER FORGET
BY AUTHORS YOU'LL ALWAYS REMEMBER

The Editors

LOVESWEPT® • 342

Iris Johansen
Magnificent Folly

BANTAM BOOKS
NEW YORK • TORONTO • LONDON • SYDNEY • AUCKLAND

MAGNIFICENT FOLLY

A Bantam Book / August 1989

LOVESWEPT® and the wave device are registered
trademarks of Bantam Books, a division of
Bantam Doubleday Dell Publishing Group, Inc.
Registered in U.S. Patent
and Trademark Office and elsewhere.

All rights reserved.
Copyright © 1989 by Iris Johansen.
Cover art copyright © 1989 by Barney Plotkin.
No part of this book may be reproduced or transmitted
in any form or by any means, electronic or mechanical,
including photocopying, recording, or by any information
storage and retrieval system, without permission in
writing from the publisher.
For information address: Bantam Books.

If you would be interested in receiving protective vinyl
covers for your Loveswept books, please write to this address
for information:

Loveswept
Bantam Books
P.O. Box 985
Hicksville, NY 11802

ISBN 0-553-22013-6

Published simultaneously in the United States and Canada

Bantam Books are published by Bantam Books, a division
of Bantam Doubleday Dell Publishing Group, Inc. Its trademark, consisting of the words "Bantam Books" and the
portrayal of a rooster, is Registered in U.S. Patent and
Trademark Office and in other countries. Marca Registrada.
Bantam Books, 666 Fifth Avenue, New York, New York 10103.

PRINTED IN THE UNITED STATES OF AMERICA

O   0 9 8 7 6 5 4 3 2 1

One

The man on the cliff was watching Cassie again.

Fear made the muscles tense in Lily Deslin's stomach. She stood on the deck of the beach house for only a few moments longer, then rushed down the steps, her pace quickening until she was running along the beach path toward Cassie's small figure playing in the surf.

She was being foolish. The man presented no threat, Lily told herself. Though he had been there on the cliff every evening for the past three days, she was sure he had not attempted to speak to Cassie. He merely had sat on the boulder on the cliff and watched her daughter play on the deserted beach.

Waiting. It seemed he was just waiting.

No. She was blowing this all out of proportion. The man was no more than a dark silhouette against the blazing scarlet of the sky. She couldn't even see his features, so how could she know that he had any purpose here other than to enjoy the spectacular view over the water of the Oregon sunset?

She knew.

"Cassie!" Lily tried to keep the panic from her voice as she crossed the last few yards separating them. "Time for supper. Come along, now."

"In a minute, Mom." Cassie kicked at the foam ruffling the waves. "It's nice now. Sort of . . ." She hesitated. "Peaceful. Don't you feel it?"

Lily forced a smile. "It will be just as nice in the morning. You're going to be as pruney as the raisins in that crazy TV commercial if you don't get out of the water." She reached down and picked up Cassie's crimson Peanuts beach towel, on which a moody Schroeder played his toy piano.

"Okay." Cassie heaved a resigned sigh and turned and trudged toward the beach. "But it won't be, you know."

Lily quickly draped the towel around Cassie's shoulders. The man was still watching. She could feel the force of his gaze as if it were a touch. "Won't be what?" she asked as she lifted Cassie's single brown braid free from the folds of the towel.

"Just as nice in the morning. You said that it would be just as nice then as it is now."

"Sorry. I guess I lost my train of thought." Lily gave her daughter a gentle push toward the path leading to the beach house and said jokingly, "Old age setting in, I reckon."

Cassie's brow creased in a thoughtful frown as she started toward the path. "I used to like mornings better here when we first came, but I don't anymore. During the last week I decided that this time of day is best. It makes me feel . . . beautiful."

Cassie *was* beautiful, Lily thought with a sudden rush of passionate tenderness. Oh, perhaps not picture-book pretty, but small and sturdy, endearingly freckled by the sun and gleaming with the golden sheen of childhood. Lily tugged teasingly at her daughter's damp braid. "I guess you're not so bad."

Cassie shook her head. "No, inside. I feel beautiful inside. Warm and sort of glowing and filled with something"—she made a helpless gesture with one hand, as if reaching for words—"special. Kind of like when I play Brahms."

"Sounds more like Mozart."

Cassie made a face. "You're making fun of me."

Lily shook her head. "No way. Just trying to make you think in more precise terms. Mozart can be peaceful. Brahms has more sweep and power. Which is it?"

"Maybe a little of both." Cassie nodded with satisfaction. "Yes, two parts Mozart and one part Brahms."

Lily's laughter pealed out. "Well, that's precise enough."

"I want to put it down on paper."

Lily tried to hide a start of surprise. Cassie hadn't done any type of composing since before the tour the year before, and Lily had begun to think she was rejecting creating anything new to avoid another onslaught of publicity such as the introduction of her first concerto had brought. "After supper," she said firmly. "Shower, supper, dishes, piano. If it's worthwhile, it will stay with you."

"But I want to—" Cassie broke off as she glanced up at her mother's face. "Shower, supper, paino," she said as a counter-offer. "You do the dishes tonight, I'll take your turn tomorrow."

"Deal."

They walked in companionable silence while the blazing scarlet of the sky turned to smoky lavender.

"You're not old," Cassie said abruptly. "Why did you say that? You'll never be old."

"Everyone grows old, Cassie."

"Not you." Cassie's clasp tightened on her hand. "You're like a Bach fugue, strong and memorable, with every note crystal-clear. You'll always be like that."

"Trust you to compare me to a fugue." Lily tried to keep the throatiness from her voice. "Are you trying to get out of doing the dishes tomorrow, too, young lady?"

Cassie glanced up, her round face alight with mischief. "If it works. Does it?"

"Nope."

"What about if I compare you to Mozart?"

Lily shook her head.

"You're pretty tough. Mozart sparkles like a diamond."

Cassie sparkled with the same many-faceted appeal, alternating between the mischief of a child and the wisdom of an adult. A feeling of profound thanksgiving suddenly surged through Lily. What had she ever done to deserve a miracle like Cassie? "I have to be tough, with a con artist like you in the house."

"I don't try to con you."

Lily raised a skeptical brow.

"No, really, I don't," Cassie insisted. "I'd never try to . . ." She giggled. "Well, almost never."

"Almost *and* never?" Lily clucked reprovingly. "Precision, love."

Cassie grimaced. "You're as bad as Professor Kozeal. Precision is boring. I like the thundering flourishes better."

"I know you do. But you have to have both in a piano concerto." Lily paused. "And in life, Cassie."

Cassie turned to look at her. "You don't," she said gravely. "You don't have any thundering flourishes. Why don't you do—"

"You provide quite enough flourishes for both of us," Lily replied, interrupting quickly. "Maybe I'm more Rachmaninoff than you think, brat."

Cassie shook her head positively. "Bach." They were approaching the weathered cedar cottage on the rise when Cassie abruptly stopped. "Wait. I forgot to say good-bye."

"What?"

Cassie started to turn around. "I forgot to say good-bye to him."

Lily stiffened. "Him?"

Cassie was waving at the shadowy figure on the cliff. As Lily watched, the man lifted his arm and waved in return. It was a casual gesture, free of any hint of menace, yet Lily felt the chill return. She kept her tone carelessly casual. "Who is he, Cassie? Has he ever spoken to you?"

"No." Cassie waved again and turned away. "But he's always there. Haven't you noticed?"

"Yes." Lily was silent a moment, trying to find the right words of caution that wouldn't frighten. "Sometimes it's not wise to be too friendly to strangers. If he ever tries to speak to you I'd like you to—"

"Oh, Mom, he's not one of those creeps you told me about who tries to give candy to kids." Cassie's tone was impatient. "He's okay."

"You can't be sure. It's always better to be careful."

"I'm sure." Cassie frowned. "He . . . likes me."

"For heaven's sake, Cassie. You just said he's never even spoken to you. How can you know that?"

Cassie's jaw was set stubbornly. "He *likes* me."

Lily knew she would get no further in trying to influence Cassie when her daughter's characteristic obstinacy was in full bloom. She would have to drop the subject and approach it later from another angle. She smiled. "What's not to like?"

A little of Cassie's belligerence eased. "He's not a creep."

"If you say so."

They walked in silence for a few moments, and they were climbing the steps when Cassie spoke again. "Andrew."

Lily glanced at her inquiringly.

"You asked if I knew who he was. His name is Andrew."

"How do you know?"

Cassie frowned in puzzlement. "I'm not sure."

Then her expression cleared. "I must have heard someone call his name sometime. Right?"

Lily nodded slowly. "That seems reasonable."

But it was the middle of September, and this section of the beach was nearly deserted. Lily had never seen anyone else on the cliff. No one at all. She shivered as she threw open the door. "Shower," she said as she gave Cassie a gentle nudge toward her room. "Then put on your pajamas and robe while I make supper. Fifteen minutes."

Cassie nodded, and a minute later the door of her room slammed behind her.

Was he still there? Lily turned slowly and looked out over the rock-strewn dunes toward the cliff. Darkness had almost entirely enveloped the sky, but she could still discern the shadowy figure on the cliff. There was no sunset to enjoy any longer, so why the hell didn't he go home?

As if in answer to her question the man rose to his feet. He stood quite still for a moment, a slim, powerful figure staring down into the darkness. Then he turned and walked away.

Lily breathed a sigh of relief before tension gripped her again. Now that he was no longer in sight he could be doing anything, going anywhere. He could even be coming down the cliff path toward the beach . . . and their cottage.

Lily slammed the door and shot the lock and then immediately felt foolish. She was being incredibly stupid. The man was probably a bespectacled accountant renting one of the cottages down the beach; perhaps he climbed the cliff every evening to watch the sunset and to get away from his wife and kids. Togetherness could be overpowering in these postage-stamp-size cottages. Yes, it was only her imagination that was inflating that solitary shadow into a figure of power and mystery.

She turned and walked briskly toward the kitchen. The unknown was always frightening. The next evening she would march up the cliff path and introduce herself to the man. If he proved a decent sort, perhaps she'd invite him to the cottage for a cup of coffee. If he was some kind of weirdo she would handle that, too, even if it meant pushing the creep off the damn cliff.

Lily smiled with satisfaction as she opened the refrigerator door and began to riffle through the vegetable crisper for lettuce and tomatoes. Eliminate the mystery and any situation could usually be handled, and some of the mystery surrounding the man on the cliff was already beginning to be dispersed. The shadow had a name.

Andrew.

"Mom, it's Professor Kozeal on the phone," Cassie called from outside the frosted-glass shower enclosure. "Shall I tell her to call you back?"

Lily grimaced. She had expected Mara Kozeal to track them down, but she'd hoped it would take longer than a week. "No, talk to her for a minute. I'll be right out."

"I was afraid you'd say that," Cassie muttered, her shadow fading away from the shower door. "She won't like it. She'll yell at me, you know."

"She never yells at you. She'll just ask questions."

"Same difference." Cassie closed the door of the bathroom behind her.

Lily smiled ruefully as she turned off the spray, slid back the door of the shower, and reached for a towel. Cassie was right. The professor's questions often sounded like the third degree, and there was no question but that she was avoiding confronting Mara Kozeal's interrogation herself. Mara believed Cassie was a child prodigy on the scale of Mozart, and would be furious to have her plans for her thwarted. Well, Lily would just have to gird herself for the battle. Mara was an exceptional teacher, and heaven knows Lily never would have been able to afford to hire anyone half so good if Mara hadn't believed in Cassie's genius enough to teach her for practically nothing, but there was no way she was going to have Cassie exploited. The national concert tour the previous year might have brought Cassie a good deal of critical acclaim, but the constant travel and papparazzi attention had given her a fine-drawn, haunted look by the time the tour had ended. Cassie possessed extraordinary talent, but she was still a little girl, with a child's needs, and Lily was not going to let her be robbed of that childhood.

She slipped on her terry-cloth robe and tied the belt before striding into the bedroom and picking up the extension. "Hello, Mara. Okay, Cassie, you can hang up now."

" 'Bye, Professor Kozeal." Cassie sounded distinctly relieved as she hurriedly hung up the extension in the living room.

Fifteen minutes later Lily replaced the receiver,

feeling as if she'd gone through a major battle. Lord, the woman was stubborn. She marched into the living room and over to the upright piano, where Cassie was sitting. "Bed," she announced. "It's after ten."

"Five minutes more." Cassie scrawled another note on the sheet in front of her. "I'll sleep late in the morning."

"You never sleep late." Lily strode across the room, took the pencil from Cassie's hand, and put it on top of the piano. "Get up at dawn and work before breakfast. That will give you all night to let the music play in your head. That always helps you."

Cassie looked longingly at the sheet already half covered with notes and then gave up. "Okay." She got off the bench and padded barefoot toward her room. "I could tell Professor Kozeal was mad. She kept muttering something about your dragging me from San Francisco to the wilds of Oregon. Did she give you hell?"

"No cursing, young lady." Lily followed her into the bedroom and pulled back the coverlet on the bed as Cassie took off her robe. "She was very understanding when I explained. She just thinks you'd be better off in San Francisco, where she can give you lessons." She made a face. "I'm sure she'd have a heart attack if she saw that upright piano I rented for you. She'd never understand why I left the Steinway in the apartment."

Cassie climbed into bed and nestled back against the pillows. "Are we going?"

Lily tucked the coverlet around Cassie's shoulders. "This cottage is kind of shabby, and there's no Steinway. Do you want to go back?"

"No."

Lily smiled as she leaned down and brushed a kiss on Cassie's temple. "Then we won't go back until we're both good and ready. I have a lease on the cottage for another five weeks."

"Good." Cassie's eyes closed. "I like it here. It's so pretty."

"Yes, it is."

Cassie yawned and turned on her side. "And the music. There's never been so much music. The wind and the sea . . ."

Lily picked up the music box on the bedside table, wound it, and set it down again. Nighttime rituals. She loved them as much as Cassie. She turned off the bedside lamp. "That's nice, love."

Cassie's voice was a drowsy murmur over the silvery melody of the music box. "Isn't it funny? It's hard to hear the music except at sunset. Then it's so clear. It's beautiful, Mom."

Lily felt a tightening in her throat. "Then you'd better go to sleep so that you can get it all down on paper tomorrow."

"Yes, tomorrow I'll . . ." Cassie's words trailed away as her breathing deepened.

Lily stood looking down at her daughter. She should go to the darkroom and get to work on those photographs. She had at least three hours' developing and enlarging to do before she could get into her own bed, and the commission for the lobby of the Landaur Building was due in two weeks. Cassie didn't need her any longer. She was sound asleep, worn out from a day of swimming and collecting shells and listening to the music no one could hear but her. Dear God, she was sweet. Honest, sensitive, mischievous, sometimes a child, sometimes an adult, always loving. If Cassie's extraordinary gift vanished the next day, she would still be a very special child. There had been a time last year when Lily had almost wished Cassie were an ordinary child, when she had seen her daughter grow quieter and more and more bewildered under the barrage of publicity that had surrounded her when the world discovered her genius. Yet how could Lily wish for the music to vanish, when it brought Cassie so much joy? There had to be a way for Cassie to have the joy of creation without being in the glare of the spotlight, and by heaven, Lily knew she would find it. It wouldn't be easy—but then, nothing had been easy since the moment she had made the decision to have a child, and she had never regretted the choice. From the moment she had felt Cassie stirring in her womb she had known only passionate gratitude and the determination to give her child all the love and care she would ever need or want.

She straightened, and then turned and moved toward the door. Well, taking care also meant financial support, and she was wasting time. Her own career as a photographer was just beginning to flourish, and it was difficult enough to make ends meet these days. There was work to be done.

Lily was quietly closing the bedroom door behind her when she heard a half-audible murmur from the bed across the room. She paused, waiting to see if Cassie would stir into wakefulness. Then, when there was no further sound, she started to swing the door shut again. The drowsy murmur came once more, clearer this time, and Lily stiffened, her hand clenching the doorknob.

"Andrew . . ."

The man wasn't on the cliff the next evening.

Lily had made sure she was available to oversee Cassie's entire stay on the beach, and had so primed herself to do battle, she felt flat when denied the opportunity. She sat down in the sand and linked her arms around her bare knees as she watched Cassie wade into the surf. "Your friend Andrew seems to have deserted us."

Cassie plopped down in the water, her fingers digging into the wet sand. An abstracted frown creased her brow as she gazed out at the scarlet streaks mirrored on the water. "What?"

"Never mind." Cassie was hearing her music, and Lily knew the child was lost to her for the time being. For a moment a wave of loneliness surged through her, before she firmly dismissed it. "It doesn't matter."

"Oh, you said . . ." Cassie buried her fingers deeper in the sand. "Andrew's around somewhere."

"How do you know?"

"Hello." The deep baritone voice behind Lily made her jump. "How are you this evening, Cassie? Ms. Deslin?"

Lily tensed as she glanced sharply over her shoulder. A tall man was walking toward them. The brilliant light of the sunset made it impossible for her to see his features, but the way he moved was unmistakable. Then, as he came closer, she felt a little of the tension ease from her rigid muscles. This young man didn't look at all threatening. He couldn't have been over twenty-four or twenty-five, and had the lean, sensual grace of one of the college men on a USC calendar. His sun-faded jeans were rolled up to reveal muscular calves, and his navy blue sweat shirt was bleached by salt and sun until its original color was scarcely discernible. Barefoot, his toes curled with evident pleasure in the softness of the sand as he strolled toward them.

"Andrew!" Cassie grinned and waved. "Oh, great. You've come down from the cliff. Why didn't you come before?"

Cassie was speaking to the man as if she had known him all her life, Lily realized with astonishment. Had Cassie not told her the truth about knowing him?

"It wasn't time. How's the concerto coming?" The man was only a few yards away now, and Lily could see that his dark blond hair was sun-streaked and his golden tan had to have been acquired from a stronger sun than shone on this Oregon coast.

"Fine." Cassie stood up and turned to face him. "How did you know that I was working on a concerto?"

"Yes, how did you know?" Lily stood up also, and there was a hint of belligerence in her stance as she dusted the sand from her shorts before taking a half step forward to stand nearer to Cassie. "You seem to be very well informed about my daughter's activities, Mr. . . ." She trailed off pointedly.

"Ramsey. Andrew Ramsey." He smiled, and his lean face was suddenly lit with an inner radiance. "Just a guess. Cassie's last concerto made her an exceptionally famous young lady. It's only reasonable that she would be working on another one."

"Is it also reasonable that a perfect stranger should recognize my daughter? Cassie isn't exactly a household name."

"It's all right, Mom," Cassie said quickly. "He's not—" She broke off and grimaced at Andrew. "She doesn't mean to be rude. She only wants to protect me. There are all kinds of weirdos running around, you know."

"I know," he said gravely. "And she's quite right to be careful of you. I'd react the same way myself."

"I don't need you to apologize for me, Cassie," Lily said in exasperation. "I think you'd better go back to the cottage until I finish talking to Mr. Ramsey."

"I told you he isn't a slime ball. You'd see that if you'd just—"

"I'll see you later, Cassie." Andrew Ramsey smiled down at the little girl. "Let me talk to your mother and straighten this out."

"Okay." Cassie started reluctantly up the beach. "But don't let her chase you away. Make her understand."

"I will."

"You'd better," Lily said as she whirled back to face him. "I don't like what's going on. Dammit, Cassie *knows* you, and she told me she had never spoken to you. My daughter has never lied to me before, and I'm mad as hell."

"Cassie didn't lie to you," Andrew Ramsey said quietly. "But yes, she does know me. Perhaps it's instinct. Haven't you ever met someone and felt you'd known him before?"

"Déjà vu? It won't wash, Mr. Ramsey. Why have you been watching Cassie? You won't deny that's what you've been doing for the last three evenings."

He shook his head. "Actually, it's been five days. You didn't notice me for the first two nights." His brown eyes were suddenly twinkling. "You've been a hell of a lot more patient than I thought you'd be. I expected to see you climbing up the path to my aerie after the second night."

"That's exactly what I was going to do this evening."

"I had an idea you might, so I thought I'd save you the trouble and come down to you. Tell me, do you really think I'm a threat to Cassie?"

"How do I know?" She met his gaze directly. "But I'm damn well going to find out. Just because you look like the clean-cut all-American boy is no sign that's what you are. I hear there are several varieties of pretty wild flowers that will grow in a toxic-waste dump."

He chuckled. "I'm glad you think I'm pretty, but I've never been compared to a toxic-waste dump before. That's an original turn of phrase." His smile faded. "What would you have done if you'd found me to be the weirdo Cassie said you suspected me of being?"

"Warned you off."

"And if I wouldn't be warned off? Would you have called the police?"

"The police aren't always effective until after a crime is committed. I would have handled it myself."

He looked surprised. "How?"

She smiled sweetly. "I have a .32 Smith and Wesson at the cottage. If I'd found you to be any sort of danger to Cassie I would have blown away that part of your anatomy on which most men place an exceedingly high value."

He chuckled. "I'd say that would have proved effective."

"Very." Her gaze searched his face. "But somehow I don't think you're a pervert."

A smile tugged at his lips. "Thank you."

"Still, you may be something almost as bad. What magazine do you write for?"

"Ah, now I'm a member of the unscrupulous papparazzi?"

"It computes, doesn't it? You know who Cassie is and you've been stalking her for almost a week."

"I haven't been stalking her."

"Then what do you call your stake-out on the cliff?"

"Pleasure." His gaze shifted to Cassie's small figure, climbing the steps of the cottage. "Enjoyment. She's pretty wonderful, isn't she?"

"Yes."

His gaze moved back to Lily's face. "You still

think I'm here to put her face on the cover of the *National Enquirer*?"

"You know too much, Mr. Ramsey, and I don't believe in coincidences."

"Andrew." He studied her face for a moment. "Poor Lily, I guess I can't blame you for acting the fierce mother tigress. Life hasn't been easy for you, has it?"

She stiffened. "And just what have you dug up in your morgue files about me?"

He shook his head, his gaze warmly sympathetic. "I'm no reporter, Lily. You're never going to see your face on a scandal sheet again. I promise you."

Again? He *did* know. She felt as if she had been punched in the stomach and had the breath knocked out of her. "Who are you?" she asked hoarsely.

"Andrew Ramsey. Would you like to see my identification?"

She gestured impatiently. "I'll accept the fact that you're telling me the truth about your name. Why are you here?"

"It was time for me to come. You've had to fight too long by yourself. I wanted to come before, but I didn't think you'd be ready for me." He shook his head. "But now it doesn't matter. Something's happened that's tossed all those reasons out the window."

Lily frowned. "You're not making sense. Are you going to tell me why you're here or not?"

He made a face. "I'm trying. I feel as awkward as hell about this. I think you're intimidating me."

She didn't believe him. She had never met anyone who displayed such serene self-confidence. "Bull."

He laughed. "I can be intimidated by people I care about."

His gaze on her face was tender, almost caressing, and she suddenly felt breathless. She took an instinctive step back, her dark eyes blazing fiercely in her taut face. "That has no bearing. I'm a stranger to you."

He shook his head wearily. "Lord, you're wary. I may be a stranger to you, but you're no stranger to me." He paused. "And neither is Cassie. I could never be a danger to Cassie, Lily."

"Fine words. How can I know that?"

He hesitated, and then answered simply, "Because I'm Cassie's father."

Two

"You're crazy," Lily said blankly.

He shook his head. "Cassie is my child. Shall I prove it? You were artificially inseminated nine years ago, in October, in the offices of Dr. Henry Slodak at Franklin University. Cassie was born May twenty-eighth of the next year. The doctor helped steer you to someone who supplied false documents showing you had been married to one Joel Deslin and that he had died.

She gazed at him in shock. "How did you find that out?" She broke off and ran her hand distractedly through her chestnut hair. "Henry Slodak is ethical. He never would have told you. I *trusted* him."

"You were right to trust him, Lily. After the insemination was successful, he told no one."

"He told you. How did you get him to do so? Money?"

"You know better than that. I realize it's not

easy for you to trust anyone, but Henry is an honorable man and a true friend to you." His tone was gentle. "He told no one after he gave you his word. As the donor I was required to give my consent. It was the arrangement we made with Henry before we set up the grant at the university."

"We?"

"The Clanad." He hesitated. "It's a sort of corporation that maintains a research foundation."

"A foundation that hires college boys to impregnant women? Lord, you must have been only seventeen or eighteen."

He chuckled. "Four years younger than you, but don't feel as if you were robbing the cradle. I was very mature for my age." He grimaced. "If it hadn't been necessary, I wouldn't have made the sperm donation. I have no liking for the clinical approach to sex."

"Henry said his donors were usually students who needed the money for tuition." She felt dazed as she tried to sift clarity from the wild jumble of thoughts whirling through her mind. "But I somehow thought you'd be . . . older."

"I'm older now. I had to play catch up."

"That's absurd. I'm almost thirty, and that makes you only twenty-five or twenty-six. You can never catch up."

"I was afraid you'd feel that way nine years ago." He added gently, "But I think you'll find I'm very mature for my age now, Lily."

"I won't find you any way at all." Her voice

was shaking. "I want you to go away and leave us alone. Cassie is mine."

"And I gave her to you."

"No." She drew a deep breath and tried to steady her voice. "There was nothing personal about it. You have no right to Cassie. Henry said there was no danger of the donor's ever trying to claim her."

"I'm laying no claim to Cassie. She's yours, Lily."

"Thank you. How very kind." Irony layered Lily's voice.

"I want to be kind to both of you. Let me help, Lily. I'm not trying to take Cassie away. I understand that I have no rights you don't give me."

"Good. So go away."

"I can't go away."

"Why not?"

"Because Cassie has rights too." He paused. "Cassie has a right to anything I have to give her, if she decides she wants it."

"She doesn't need you. *I* don't need you."

He didn't answer.

"Have you been meeting Cassie behind my back and trying to influence her?"

Hurt flickered across his face. "I said I hadn't spoken to her. Perhaps when you get to know me better, you'll find I don't lie."

"I have no intention of getting to know you better." Her hands clenched into fists at her sides. "I've gotten along without help from anyone for the last nine years, and I certainly don't need any help now. Henry never should have told you where to find us."

"Henry had no choice. Besides, he likes you. He hated to see you struggling all these years." Andrew lifted one shoulder in a half shrug. "But he knew you wouldn't accept any help. Your wounds had to heal first, and you had to be sure you didn't need help before you could allow yourself to accept it."

"Be *quiet*. I don't know what you think you're doing here, but I wish you'd go away. Neither Cassie nor I need or want you." She turned and started down the beach.

"I hope you're wrong." Andrew's voice held a note of wistfulness as it followed her. "Dear Lord, I hope you're wrong."

Her steps quickened until she was almost running as she fled up the path toward the beach house.

"She wouldn't listen?"

Andrew turned his gaze from Lily, to see Gunner Nilsen coming down the cliff path. Andrew smiled ruefully at his friend. "I knew she wouldn't, but I had to try. She was getting frightened, and I couldn't stand it. She's had enough fear and hurt in her life."

"And you haven't?" Gunner asked. "The pain is so great that just one of those sessions you go through would traumatize any member of the Clanad."

Andrew shook his head. "That's different. I'm not the victim. It's my choice."

Gunner was silent a moment. "You could go underneath."

"No!" Andrew said violently. "It has to be on her terms. She deserves fair treatment. Honesty."

"I suppose she does." Gunner clapped a hand on Andrew's shoulder. "Come on, Quenby will be waiting, and you promised to call Jon this evening. You can't do anything more tonight. Lily's been among the walking wounded for the last ten years, so you can't expect her to trust you right away. Give her a chance to absorb what you've told her. You can see her in the morning."

"If she's still here in the morning." Andrew's gaze went back to the beach house. "She's frightened. Why is she so damned scared of me?"

"You know why," Gunner said. "Cassie. You should have let someone else be the donor."

"I couldn't. Not from the first time I saw Lily." Andrew turned away and fell into step with Gunner. "She's different now."

Gunner nodded. "She's a damn beautiful woman."

Lily was more than beautiful, Andrew thought. The first time he'd seen her she had been nineteen years old, a girl with long, gleaming chestnut hair, huge dark eyes, and an appealing, dewy-eyed freshness. Her hair was shorter now, barely reaching her shoulders before turning under in a shining bell. She had ripened and matured and, though she had lost that youthful sheen, she had gained character, humor, understanding. Her tall, slim body seemed more lithe and womanly, and she moved with decision and purpose. Her breasts were more voluptuous, her long, slim legs tanned and shapely.

Andrew felt a familiar stirring in his groin and tried to stop it. Not now. He mustn't let sex interfere with what he had to do. His lips twisted. Easy to say when Lily was out of sight, but it hadn't been so simple when he had been standing in front of her and imagining what it would be like to have her beneath him in the sand. To watch her face as he moved between her thighs, to have those long legs clasp him lovingly, desperately, in a fever of—

"Andrew."

Andrew glanced at Gunner and then grimaced as he saw his friend's amused smile. "Dammit, stop grinning like a gargoyle."

"Then stop being so blasted transparent." Gunner chuckled. "You're so hot for her, it's obvious you have no guard at all." His gaze shifted pointedly to the lower part of Andrew's body. "Very obvious."

"Maybe I shouldn't have brought you with me. I'm not that transparent to everyone."

"A blind man could read you, at the moment." Gunner sobered. "If you hadn't asked me to come, Jon still would have sent me. This isn't your personal business only, Andrew. Cassie belongs to the Clanad, and the Clanad protects its own."

"I can protect Cassie."

"Maybe. But it's not your job. I'm the trouble-shooter. Your value extends in other directions."

"You can't believe the possibility of danger is very strong if you brought Quenby along."

"Quenby can be stubborn. She cares about you." Gunner added, "And, since she's very good with children, I thought it might be just as well to have her nearby if we have to take Cassie away from Lily for a while."

"We can't do that."

"We will, if it means keeping Cassie safe." Gunner's tone was implacable. "And you know damn well that you'll sanction it if it comes down to the wire."

"Maybe it won't," Andrew said as he started up the cliff path. "If I have enough time."

Gunner didn't answer as he followed Andrew up the trail. He didn't have to state what they both knew as fact.

Time was running out.

"Cassie, I'm not going to discuss it. Mr. Ramsey's not going to be invited here and, if he comes to the beach again, you're not to speak to him." Lily tried to keep her voice from trembling. Lord, this was hard. Why wouldn't Cassie give up? Ever since Lily had walked through the door, Cassie had been like a terrier clinging to a slipper, on the subject of Andrew. Now, after a long argument with many tears, Cassie's disappointment had turned to anger. "You don't even know this man. There's no reason for this temper tantrum."

"Why?" Cassie asked. "It's stupid of you not to tell me why. You've never shut me out like this before. You've always explained."

"You'll just have to accept that I'm doing what's best."

Cassie shook her head so hard, her brown braid bounced. "You're not doing what's best. Andrew won't hurt me. Andrew won't hurt either of us. Why can't you see it?"

"Cassie, that's enough. Now, go take your shower while I fix supper."

Cassie glared at her across the room.

"Cassie!"

Cassie whirled on her heel and strode toward her bedroom. "I don't want any supper."

Lily couldn't stand it. "Wait." She swallowed to ease the tightness in her throat. "I realize this is difficult for you to understand, but you know I'd never do anything to hurt you. Andrew is a stranger. He can't be all that important to you." She forced herself to smile. "Suppose I let you stay up an extra hour tonight to work on your concerto."

Cassie glanced over her shoulder, her hazel eyes glistening with tears. "I don't want to work tonight. There's no music." She entered her bedroom and shut the door behind her.

But she had been hearing the music earlier, while she had been sitting in the surf, Lily thought. Before Andrew Ramsey strode down from his damn eagle's perch, she and Cassie had been serene and happy. Now there was nothing but anger and turbulence. Why the hell hadn't he stayed away from them? The last thing Lily needed in her life was a kid who had suddenly decided he should embrace the responsiblities of fatherhood. Ramsey couldn't be long out of college, and, in spite of the tough virility of his physique, there was something radiantly youthful about him. His confidence seemed founded on an inner strength rather than worldly experience. Well, Andrew Ramsey could just go get his worldly experience somewhere else.

Pain tore through Lily as she remembered how Cassie had glared at her a few minutes before. Dear heaven, Cassie had never looked at her like that. She felt almost sick with misery. Cassie would get over it, she told herself. By the next day her daughter would have forgotten Andrew Ramsey.

No, she was lying to herself. Cassie wouldn't forget. Cassie seldom forgot anything, and she was always steadfast in her loyalties. By an odd quirk of fate she had fixed her loyalty on Andrew Ramsey, and she would cling to it even if it meant being torn between Andrew and her mother.

Lily moved toward the front door, blinded by tears. Her stomach was so tied into knots, she knew she wouldn't be able to eat, and there was no way she could go to bed and sleep. A moment later she was standing on the wooden deck, looking down at the moon-silvered surf crashing against the rocks on the beach below.

"Let me talk to her."

Lily jerked around to face the flight of stairs leading to the deck.

"I wasn't going to see you two until tomorrow." Andrew was coming up the steps. "But then I remembered Cassie, and how she was bound to react. She's upset, isn't she?"

"Yes, damn you." Lily clasped her hands tightly together. "Why the hell did you come here? Everything was fine before you showed up."

He was now standing before her on the deck, gazing down at her face. "And you're in pain too. Damn, I'm sorry, Lily." He took an impulsive step forward. "Let me help to—" He stopped and slowly shook his head. "Not yet."

"You can help by going away."

"That's no answer. You're very close to Cassie. You know how she thinks."

"But you don't. You don't know anything about her. She's not a toy you can take up because you want to play father, then drop when she begins to bore you."

"It's not like that, Lily. Trust me."

"I can't trust you. I have a daughter lying in bed probably crying herself to sleep, and she won't even let me comfort her." The tears brimmed helplessly in Lily's eyes. "She's never turned away from me before. She's always loved me and known I love—" Her voice broke, and she was forced to stop. She was silent a moment, and her voice was still uneven when she was able to continue. "Please go away and leave us alone."

"Can't you see I can't do that?" The pain threading Andrew's voice was so intense, it startled her. "I have to help. Let me see her, Lily."

"No."

"Please." Andrew's features were strained in the moonlight, the flesh drawn tightly on the bones of his face. "I *need* to help. I can't leave you like this.

Let me talk to her for five minutes and try to make it right between you."

"And tell her you're her father?"

"No." His grave gaze was fixed on her face. I don't have that option until I earn it or you give it to me. I'll just make her understand." He smiled coaxingly. "I'll even make sure she eats her dinner."

Lily looked at him in surprise. "How do you know she didn't?"

"Well, you said she was upset. Naturally, I assumed . . ." He gestured impatiently. "That's not important. Do you want Cassie to have a bad night?"

"Of course not, but I don't want you—" She stopped when she realized what she was about to say. Was she so selfish, she would prefer Cassie to be miserable just because she couldn't be the one to comfort her?

"Cassie's the most important thing in your life; it's only reasonable that you would resent outside interference." Andrew's tone was infinitely gentle.

"You're very perceptive." She looked him directly in the eyes. "I do resent you. If I let you talk to Cassie now, it doesn't mean that I won't try to get rid of you as soon as possible."

Andrew smiled sadly. "I know, Lily."

She turned away from him and looked out over the sea. "Five minutes. First door to the left."

"Right. I'll leave the doors open, so that you can hear I'm not maligning you to her."

She heard the door behind her open, Andrew's steps, then the knock on Cassie's door.

In exactly five minutes she heard his laughing

farewell as he left Cassie's room. Cassie was laughing, too, and the sound sent a pang through Lily that was half relief and half envy. A moment later, Andrew stood beside her on the deck.

"She told me to ask you if she could have a cheeseburger for supper." A faint smile touched his lips. "And potato chips instead of a green vegetable. I think she's trying to wring everything she can out of this situation."

"She's capable of it." Lily turned to face him. "What did you tell her?"

"Nothing you wouldn't want me to tell her." He paused, and his hands reached out and closed on the railing of the deck. "But I did say I'd stick around and hope you'd let us become better friends."

Lily stiffened warily.

"Who knows? Maybe Cassie will find my company boring," he said lightly. "They say familiarity breeds contempt."

"Not bloody likely." Lily's lips tightened. "I think you've hypnotized her."

"Instinct." His hands loosened their grip on the railing, and one finger traced the rough pattern of the wood. "If you're right about me, maybe I'll be the one to grow bored and walk away. Either way, you'll be rid of me." His gaze narrowed on her face. "Or perhaps you don't think I'm that immature anymore."

She didn't know what to think. One moment Andrew seemed boyish, and in the next she glimpsed a maturity beyond the youthful radiance of him that startled her. "I don't understand what you are."

"Then find out. Let me get to know Cassie. Let me get to know *you*, Lily." He took a step closer, and one finger gently touched her cheek. "You won't regret it. I'll never hurt you."

Yet the touch of his finger on her cheek brought a burning sensation close to pain, she thought dazedly. His gaze was holding her own with mesmerizing intensity. She took a deep breath and moistened her lips with her tongue. "I'd never let you hurt me." She took a step back and his hand fell away from her face. "This is crazy. I don't know what to think. I don't even know if you're really who you say you are. What proof do I have?"

"None." Andrew thought for a moment. "Call Henry. I understand you've kept in touch with him over the years. Ask him for the name of Cassie's donor."

"He told me the names of the donors were kept confidential."

"He won't give you the same answer now." He asked curiously, "Just what did he tell you about the donor?"

"Not much, except that he was young, healthy, and intelligent, and absolutely stable mentally."

He nodded. "I can see how the last would be important to you." He smiled. "I'm still all those things, Lily. If you accepted me as a father for your child, don't you think you could take the chance on me as a friend?"

"That's different."

"A different kind of intimacy?" He took a step

closer, and his finger touched her lower lip. "Intimacy is good, Lily. I'm not Tait Baldor."

The name struck through her like a sword, piercing the dreamy languor Andrew was weaving about her. She stepped back again. "I don't want to talk about Tait Baldor."

Andrew nodded. "All right, we won't discuss him now, but we'll have to talk about him sometime."

"No, we won't." She moved decisively toward the front door. "My past is my own business and none of yours," she said over her shoulder.

"But I'm part of your past, Lily." His soft words followed her. "And your present is very much my business. I'll be down at the beach at four tomorrow afternoon. I'm telling you in case you want to be there to protect Cassie from me." He paused. "But I hope you believe now that I would never hurt her."

She turned to face him, her gaze troubled. "I don't . . . know. Perhaps you wouldn't mean to hurt her, but Cassie is very sensitive, and for some reason she seems to have taken a shine to you."

"Like to like." He grinned. "Still, I think you'd feel more secure with me tomorrow if you were sure I was Cassie's father. I'd like you to call Henry tonight and ask him about me. Will you do that?"

"Perhaps." She didn't look at him again as she closed the door behind her. She leaned back against the door feeling strangely drained. There was no reason for her to have this reaction to Andrew Ramsey. His voice had been gentle, his words persuasive and not threatening. Yet she felt as if she had been in a losing struggle with a titantic personality. She believed she had taught herself to be a fair judge of character, but Andrew Ramsey was an enigma to her.

"Can I have my cheeseburger?"

Lily straightened to see Cassie grinning at her from the doorway of her room. She was dressed in her pajamas, and there was no hint of antagonism in her expression. Lily felt a rush of relief. "I don't see why not."

"And potato chips?"

Lily grinned back at her. "Potato chips." She paused. "After you eat your vegetables."

Cassie sighed. "Andrew said I was pushing it."

Lily's smile faded. "I'm not going to lie to you, Cassie. I haven't made a decision about your friend Andrew."

"I know you haven't. Andrew said we had to give you plenty of time." Cassie's bunny slippers shuffled on the wooden floor as she came toward the kitchen. "He explained it all to me."

"Andrew seems good at explanations," Lily said dryly.

"Oh, he is. Andrew makes things clear as glass. You'll see that when you get to know him." Cassie glanced over her shoulder. "Do I still get that extra hour at the piano?"

"I thought you said the music was gone."

"It's back now." Cassie's words trailed behind her as she entered the kitchen. "Andrew brought it back."

How had Andrew managed to capture Cassie so

completely in so short a time? Lily wondered with helpless exasperation. She started across the living room toward the kitchen even as Cassie suddenly appeared again and dashed toward her.

"Cassie, what on earth is—"

"I forgot." Cassie threw her arms around her mother's waist in an enthusiastic bear hug that robbed Lily of breath, her cheek pressing hard at Lily's midriff. "I love you, Mom."

"Do you?" Lily felt as if a magic ointment had been smoothed over the rawness of a wound. "I love you, too, Cassie." Her arms tightened around her child's warm, sturdy body. "So much. I only want to do what's best for both of us."

"I know." Cassie looked up and smiled. "Me too."

Lily's lips twisted. "And do I have Mr. Ramsey to thank for this display of affection?"

Cassie shook her head. "He didn't tell me to do anything. He just said that if you love someone you ought to tell them . . . because sometimes they forget."

"Very wise advice," Lily said slowly. She gave Cassie another hug and pushed her away. "Will you make the hamburger patties, love? I have a telephone call to make. It shouldn't take long."

"Sure. Professor Kozeal?"

"No." Lily turned to the phone on the pine table beside the Early American sofa. "I have to call an old friend I knew before you were born."

When Lily took Cassie down for her swim the

next day, Andrew was sitting in exactly the same spot where she had left him the previous evening.

Cassie ran on ahead to meet him, and Lily watched them curiously. This was Cassie's father, who had given her those bright hazel eyes. Instead of Andrew's dark gold hair or Lily's chestnut, Cassie's was a sandy compromise. Together Lily and Andrew had made Cassie what she was. It was strange to realize that her own body had protected and nurtured this stranger's seed.

Andrew's gaze lifted to meet hers over Cassie's head. She inhaled sharply and stopped as if struck. Overpoweringly sexual, invading, stirring. Lust.

Then his gaze quickly lowered to Cassie again, and he displayed only affection and amusement.

But Lily hadn't imagined the emotion she had seen there.

Cassie was running out into the surf, and Andrew watched her for a moment before turning again to face Lily. "I blew it, didn't I? Gunner always said I was transparent as hell. You don't have to stand there as if I turned you to stone. There's nothing to be afraid of."

Lily started toward him. "I'm not afraid of you."

He gazed at her skeptically. "You're shaking in your shoes. You want to run away and hide."

"Nonsense." She wanted to wipe her damp palms on her shorts but forced them to remain at her sides. "Why should I be nervous?"

"Because now you know I want to go to bed with you," he said simply. "No, you know I'm crazy to go to bed with you and you're afraid I'll make you crazy enough to do it."

Lily tried to laugh. "I'm not one of the coeds you probably had panting after you. I'm a mother who has responsibilities and who—"

"Put her sexual feelings in the deep freeze before Cassie was born." Andrew finished her sentence. "Well, it's time somebody pushed the defrost button, Lily."

"You?" Lily deliberately injected a note of scorn in her voice. "Hardly."

"Me." For the first time she detected a steely determination in the softness of his voice. "Definitely me. Did you call Henry last night?"

"Yes."

"Then you know I'm not someone who's going to hurt you. What did he say?"

"That you were probably the most remarkable man he'd ever met and that I should trust you."

"And were you going to trust me before you found out I wanted you?"

She was silent a moment before admitting reluctantly, "Yes."

"Then nothing is changed."

"Everything is changed."

"What? I'm going to seduce you, not rape you. I understand the word *no*." His eyes twinkled with sudden mischief. "I just want you to learn how to say yes. Since we're going to have Cassie for a chaperon most of the time, it's going to be difficult as hell for me even to get the chance to teach you."

"You're treating me as if I'm some kind of emotional retard," Lily said. "I assure you I'm perfectly normal and far from frigid."

Andrew shook his head. "I know, love. You're

very passionate, and that's the problem. You're afraid of losing control again with any man, after what Baldor did to you." He smiled coaxingly as his gaze moved over her face caressingly. "But you're safe with me. You'll always be safe with me."

Incredibly, she found herself wanting to believe him. His expression was loving, his eyes clear and free from lies. She tore her gaze from his own to speak haltingly. "I think you'd better go away. Perhaps you've concocted some kind of idiotic scenario where you and I and Cassie live happily ever after, but when you grow up you'll find there aren't any fairy tales in this day and age. What happened nine years ago was both clinical and final and has nothing to do with the present or the future."

He chuckled. "I wish you'd stop referring to me as if I were Joe College—and slightly immature, at that. You'd be surprised how long ago I received my degree." He sobered. "When we grow older, Lily, we have to create our own fairy tales out of the materials at hand."

She shook her head. "Life isn't like that."

"It can be." He held out his hand. "Sit beside me"

Exasperated, she stood looking down at him. "Why won't you go away? I've told you it's no good."

"And I've told you I'll be patient and not rush you. I won't even touch you unless you say it's okay. I just want to be with you and talk to you. You've never had anyone with whom to share Cassie, and I think you're going to like having someone to talk to who is as interested in her as you. You're a very giving woman, Lily." He held her gaze. "Children grow up so soon, and shared experiences are richer. Sit down, love."

She found herself dropping down beside him on the sand and then wondered why on earth she had given in to his plea. She hadn't intended to stay. She had intended to call Cassie and return to the house. She could still do it, she assured herself. She'd just stay a few minutes and then get up and leave Andrew. "Who's Gunner?"

Andrew looked at her with sudden wariness.

"The man who said you were transparent."

"Gunner Nilsen, an old friend. He and his wife and I are sharing a cabin about a half mile from the crest of that cliff."

"Oh, then Cassie was right."

Andrew looked at her inquiringly.

"She didn't know how she knew your name was Andrew. She thought she must have heard someone call you."

Andrew's lids lowered to veil his eyes. "That sounds reasonable."

"I'm glad you're not claiming it was daughterly instinct," Lily said dryly. "That would be carrying it a bit far."

"No, I'm not claiming daughterly instinct." His gaze shifted to Cassie. "She's really beautiful, isn't she?" The expression on Andrew's face was also beautiful, Lily thought in bemusement. "Has she always liked the water?"

"No, she was actually afraid of it before we took lessons together at the YWCA last year."

"Tell me about it." Andrew settled back on one elbow. "Tell me all about her. I've missed a hell of a lot, haven't I?"

For an instant Lily thought he was trying to lull her into a sense of security, but there was no mistaking the wistfulness of Andrew's expression. He *had* missed a lot, she thought suddenly. All of those precious years when Cassie was a baby and then a toddler, the moment when she had discovered her music, the laughter at her second birthday party when she'd plunged both chubby hands into the icing of the chocolate cake. Lily had all those memories, but he had nothing.

She was silent for a long moment, and then, slowly, she began to tell him about Cassie.

Three

"How's Cassie's concerto coming?" Andrew asked as he wadded up the tinfoil wrapper from his ham sandwich and threw it into the surf.

"Very well." She frowned. "You shouldn't throw refuse into the ocean. It's polluted enough."

"Sorry, you're right. I didn't think." He bit into his sandwich before looking up with a grin. "Shall I swim out and get it?"

Lily tilted her head quizzically. "What would you do if I said yes?"

"I'd swim out and get it."

Lily threw back her head and laughed. "You probably would do it. You're completely impossible, do you know that?"

"I've been accused of it before." He took another bite. "But there's a method to my madness. Ladies are said to like flamboyant, romantic gestures."

"Really?"

"You needn't raise your eyebrows at me. It's

true. I'd also get soaked to the skin, and you're so softhearted you'd feel obliged to take me home and dry me off. It would actually be a very clever move on my part."

"And completely calculated."

The smile left his lips. "No," he said quietly. "I was joking. I'd do it because you wanted me to do it. I'll always give you what you want, if it's within my power, Lily."

She had known he was joking. In the past two weeks she had discovered there was nothing calculating about Andrew. She looked quickly away down the beach at Cassie, who was putting the finishing touches on an enormous sand castle. "Impossible. Utterly impossible."

Impossibly quixotic, impossibly honest, impossibly stubborn, impossibly lovable. She carefully shifted her thoughts from the dangerous path where they were wandering. "You make me feel a hundred years old and positively maternal."

"No, I don't." He finished the sandwich and reached for the Styrofoam cup of coffee beside him on the beach rug. "Oh, sometimes, maybe." He lifted the cup to his lips and looked at her over the rim. "But most of the time I turn you on."

Her gaze flew back to his face in surprise. It was the first time he had said anything in the least sexually oriented since that day on the beach almost fourteen days before. He had been stimulating, companionable, entertaining, and she had gradually allowed herself to relax in his company. "I've changed my mind. Not utterly impossible— you're utterly egotistical."

"Nope." He set the cup down before stretching out full length and closing his eyes. "You've been fighting against it, but I've been growing on you."

"And how do you deduce that?"

"Instinct. I have infallible instincts, remember?"

"I'm getting very tired of hearing about your instincts."

"But you're not getting tired of me." He half opened his eyes and gazed up at her. "You like me, don't you?"

"You're . . . amusing."

"And you'd miss me if I went away?"

"Maybe."

"And you think I'm sexy?"

She made a face at him. "I'm not about to touch that question."

"Touching is good. I wish you'd touch me." He closed his eyes again. His voice was so soft, she had to strain to hear it. "I think about touching you all the time."

Dear heavens, he was beautiful. The faded jeans clung to his long, powerful thighs and rode low on his slim hips. He had taken off his shirt to get some sun when he'd first sat down beside her that afternoon, and now his reclining position pulled the muscles of his stomach taut as they flowed into the corded strength of his chest and shoulders. She had a sudden urge to put her hand on that flat stomach and feel the muscles contract. Warmth stung her cheeks as she looked quickly back at Cassie. "Then you should think about something more productive."

"I'm hoping it will be *very* productive. What are you thinking about?"

She had been thinking how gorgeously tough he looked and wondering how many women had thought the same thing. "Don't your damned instincts tell you?"

"Let me see." His lids lifted to reveal brown eyes sparkling with humor. "You're lusting after me again. Why don't you give in to it, Lily? I guarantee I'll be a pushover."

"I was not lusting after you. I was just wondering where you got the great tan."

"The Clanad is based in Sedikhan. It's principally desert country."

"You work for a foreign corporation?"

"International."

"What does the Clanad produce?"

"Lots of things," Andrew said vaguely. "It's sort of hard to explain. Why do you want to know?"

"You never talk about your work. What do you do for this Clanad corporation?"

"It's kind of difficult to describe. I guess you could say I fix things when they break down."

"Computers?"

He shook his head. "I told you it was a difficult job to describe."

"Well, they seem to give you plenty of time off. Corporations don't usually give such long vacations to new employees, even if—"

"But I'm not new." He sat up and reached for his cream-colored shirt. "I'm an old and trusted employee. They want to keep me happy."

"Old?" she asked dryly. "Then you must have started working for them when you were in high school."

"Something like that." He started to button his shirt. "You seem to have a hang-up because I'm younger than you. Four years shouldn't make a difference." He grinned impishly. "Particularly as I'm such a jaded man of the world these days."

No one could be less jaded than Andrew, Lily thought with sudden aching tenderness. He lived each moment with the same zest and curiosity Cassie did. "No way. Sometimes I think I should send you out to play in the sand, the way I do Cassie."

His smile faded. "There you go again. I'm not a kid, Lily. If you want to build defenses, you can't base them on those four years. I'm no inexperienced boy who has a fixation of an older woman. I think sex is great and I have strong appetites, but that isn't what this is all about. I want much more from you." His lips tightened. "And, by God, I'll have it."

"Andrew . . ." She gazed at him helplessly. "Go away. I'll hurt you. I don't have anything left to give. He drained me."

"Baldor? He may have almost destroyed you, but you were too strong for him. You just needed time to recover and heal." He was suddenly on his knees beside her. "You're ready to come alive again, Lily. Don't be afraid. Let me help."

He was burning, blazing, with nearly irresistible intensity. She found herself swaying toward him as if drawn into the center of a tornado. "You don't know what you're talking about," she whispered.

"Yes, I do." He framed her cheeks with his hands and gazed down into her eyes. "Do you like me?"

She didn't answer.

"Don't hide it. Tell me."

"Yes."

"Do you think I want to hurt you?"

"No, but—"

"Shhh. We're making progress." He smiled down at her with radiant sweetness. "Now the big one. Do you want me?"

"I told you I didn't." She moistened her lips with her tongue and, since he continued to stare down at her, finally burst out, "Yes, dammit, but it doesn't mean anything."

He laughed joyously as he gave her a quick, exuberant kiss. "The hell it doesn't."

His lips were hard, firm, and warm, and she had wanted them to linger. She unconsciously tilted her head back, seeking more. He smelled of clean soap and fresh sea air as the warmth of his body reached out to enfold her.

"When?" he asked softly. "Tell me when, love."

"We can't. Cassie—"

"Tonight. After Cassie goes to sleep. I'll be here on the beach. Will you come?" He drew a shaky breath. "Lord, I want you to come. There are so many things I want to do with you. I want my hands on your breasts. I want to come into you and hear you cry out when I please you. I want to—"

"No . . . I don't want to hear it." His words were a heady aphrodisiac. She could feel the cotton of her shirt tauten as her breasts swelled.

"Just once," he said coaxingly. "Just come to me once, and if you're disappointed I'll never ask you to come again. Just once, Lily. You're a passionate woman, and you need this. You need *me*."

A liquid burning tingled between her thighs, causing her muscles to clench. "It's not so simple."

"It can be. If you change your mind after you come to me, I'm not going to force you. Come tonight, and if you decide you'd like it, then let me love you."

If she decided she wanted him? She was melting, trembling, aching with need right at that moment, and he'd scarcely touched her. "It's all wrong. You have everything all mixed up. You don't really want me."

A smile tugged at his lips. "Lily, my love, if I don't want you, then why am I going to have to hightail it out of here before Cassie glances over and notices something most peculiar about my physique?"

"It's just some sort of romantic fixation," she said desperately. "I'm the mother of your child, and the situation intrigues you."

"Then let me get the fixation out of my system in the most pleasant possible way."

"You said this wasn't about sex."

"It's not, but sex is a way I can get closer to you."

"No, that's not—" She broke off as she scrambled to her feet. "I have to get Cassie. The tide's beginning to come in."

He stood up slowly. "You're running away."

"You bet I am." She quickly scooped up the thermos, plates, and cups and dumped them into the rattan picnic basket. "You're a menace. What did you major in at good old Franklin University? Seduction?"

"I never said I attended Franklin." His tone was abstracted as he picked up the beach rug and started to fold it. "Will you come tonight?"

"I have to get Cassie." She refused to meet his gaze as she picked up the basket, and spoke quickly, almost feverishly. "I should have told her to build that beautiful sand castle closer to the cliff. She's going to be heartbroken when the tide washes it away."

"No, she won't. She's finished it. It belongs to her now. The feeling of creation can't be taken away from her."

"Even if the product of her creative labor is destroyed? Don't be silly. It's pure folly to build something knowing it's going to be destroyed." She turned to face him. "Can't you see that?"

He shook his head. "You build, you enjoy, you let go." He paused. "But you never really lose anything. The experience is always a part of you."

"Cassie!" she called. "It's time to go home." They watched the little girl as she waved in acknowledgment before gathering her pail and shovels.

"You don't believe me," Andrew said.

"You're a romantic," Lily said crisply as she took the beach rug from him. "I'm a realist. Never the twain shall meet. Can't you see what a disaster any relationship between us would be?"

"No." He waved good-bye to Cassie and started across the beach toward the path leading up the cliff. "I'll be here tonight."

"I won't come."

He didn't look back. "I'll still be here."

She wouldn't go down to the beach.

Her hands gripped her upper arms as she gazed down at the crashing surf. There was no question about her doing anything so foolish as to start a sexual relationship with a man like Andrew.

She turned, quickly crossed the deck, and entered the cottage. She shot the bolt on the front door and turned off the lamps. If he was watching the cottage, he would see the lights go out, know she had no intention of coming to him, and go away.

She peeped in at Cassie to make sure she was sleeping soundly, then went to her own room and closed the door. Without turning on the light she crossed to the window and flipped open the blind.

Darkness. No moon-silvered beach that night. Even if Andrew were waiting down there, she would not be able to see him from this window.

Andrew was there. She knew he was.

She could race to the beach, into his arms, and he would pull her down in the sand to move over her. He would smell clean and salty, as he had that afternoon; his body would be strong, eager, even frantic.

Lord, what was she thinking? She was no dog in heat. She was a mature woman, who made decisions with her mind, not with her glands. So she needed a man. It didn't have to be this man. Perhaps Andrew was right about her coming alive again, but it didn't mean she had to involve herself with a man who was as dangerous to her as Andrew.

Dangerous. The realization came as a shock. Andrew was gentleness and sweet, coaxing words, glowing youthfulness and blatant sexuality. Yet beneath that shimmering exterior she had always been subliminally aware of an iron core of determination that would never relent.

Well, she would not relent either. She took off her cotton robe and dropped it on the rocking chair beside the window. Then she strode briskly to the double bed and slipped beneath the crisp cotton sheets. She would close her eyes and forget about Andrew. She turned on her side, trying not to notice the heavy ripeness of her breasts, the aching emptiness between her thighs.

She would go to sleep and forget how Andrew had looked lolling on the beach rug, his fair hair disheveled, his body tanned and hard and beautiful.

She moved restlessly as lust surged through her.

She mustn't go down to the beach.

"I missed you," Andrew said quietly as he threw a pebble out into the surf. "I stayed here a long time thinking about you."

"I told you I wouldn't come." She nervously clasped her fingers together over her knees. "I wondered whether you'd show up this afternoon."

"Because you didn't sleep with me?" He shook his head. "Being with you and Cassie means so much to me. It doesn't matter if I hurt with wanting you. I told you this wasn't about sex."

"You could have fooled me." She could have bitten her tongue as his gaze shifted to her face and he gave her a slow smile. "And you needn't look so satisfied. What I want isn't always what I permit myself to have."

"Did you have a bad night?" he asked, then spoke without waiting for her response. "Me too. But maybe we'll both have a better one tonight. I'll be here every night, Lily." His voice softened to velvet persuasiveness. "Every single night." He jumped to his feet. "I'm going down to play with Cassie."

"I suppose you're going to help her build another sand castle," she said irritably.

"Maybe." He rolled up his jeans and stripped off his T-shirt. "Want to join us?"

She shook her head. "I've told you my views on sand castles. I'll sit here and watch."

He turned and ran like an exuberant child down the sandy, rock-strewn beach toward Cassie.

Lily shifted restlessly on the bed.

She would *not* get up and go to him. She had resisted the temptation for the last four nights, and she could hold out this night too.

She wouldn't think about him.

She would squelch her erotic thoughts about him.

She wouldn't lie awake until dawn again.

Dear heaven, she wanted to go to him.

"Do you ever dream, Lily?"

"Sometimes." She wished he would move away. She could feel the heat his body was emitting, and it caused the now-familiar weakness to attack her limbs. "Doesn't everybody?"

"I used to dream a lot when I was a kid. Not so much lately. I had a dream last night that you came to me and you let me love you."

"Go away." Her tone was thick with tension. "It's not going to happen."

"It's got to happen. It's the next step. All you have to do is come to me. Then all that tension will be gone and you'll be able to be comfortable with me again."

She moved away from him. "If you'd only stop talking about it, I'd be comfortable again."

"No, you wouldn't. It's too late. Would you like to hear about my dream? It was very explicit. Definitely X-rated."

"No!" She buried her face on her drawn-up knees. She wanted to get up and leave him, but she knew she wouldn't move as long as he was next to her. As an addict craved his drug, so she had come to crave his presence, the sight of him, even the frustration of her need for him. What the hell was happening to her? "Why don't you go talk to Cassie?"

His smile was lovingly sweet, but his words were relentless as he murmured, "Later, Lily. Right now I want to tell you about my dream. You were naked, and your breasts were beautiful in the moonlight. I put my mouth on your nipple and I could feel it harden as my tongue touched it."

Her nipples were hardening just then, and she

could feel his gaze on the front of her T-shirt, watching the transformation.

"Yes," he said. "Just like that, Lily. You bent over me, and I held your breasts in my hands while I sucked and nipped at those pretty—"

"Shut up," Lily said hoarsely. "I don't want to hear this."

"No, but you want to feel it." Andrew smiled. "And you won't let me touch you, so I have to dream—and you have to listen to my dreams."

"I don't have to listen to anything."

"Then get up and walk away, Lily," Andrew said gently. He leaned back on one elbow, his gaze on the evidence of her body's betrayal of her will revealed by her clinging T-shirt. "If you don't walk away, you're most certainly going to hear the rest of my dream in great detail."

She didn't *want* to leave him, dammit. Why couldn't he just be quiet?

"Then I rolled you over in the sand and moved between those gorgeous long legs of yours, but I didn't enter you right away, love. I wanted to play for a while, so I opened your legs and . . ."

His words went on for a long time, each sentence creating pictures that made heat build within her until she could scarcely bear it. She should have gotten up and walked away from him.

She sat there, not looking at him, listening.

It rained that night, a hard, gusty downpour that swept the surf against the rocks of the shore. Even Andrew wouldn't be stubborn enough to wait for her on the beach in weather like this, Lily assured herself as she looked out her bedroom window. It would be crazy for anyone to be out in such weather.

But Andrew would be there waiting for her.

Because the stupid man was quixotic and impossible and utterly tenacious, and it only served him right if he caught a chill and ended up in the hospital with pneumonia.

A bolt of fear shot through her, exasperation and emotional turmoil in its wake. She certainly didn't care if he got sick. Then he'd have to leave her and Cassie alone.

Another jagged burst of lightning split the darkness, followed immediately by a crash of thunder.

Cassie . . .

No, the storm wouldn't disturb Cassie. She always slept so soundly, a freight train could have rolled through the house without waking her.

The only victim of the storm would be that idiot down on the beach.

Maybe the lightning would strike him or he would slip on the rain-slickened rocks and hit his head.

Stupid. So damned stupid.

Then Lily was running from her room, across the living room, toward the front door.

Puddles of rain had already formed on the deck, soaking her slippered feet as she flew through them and down the steps. She lost the slippers a moment later as she dashed down the incline toward the sandy beach.

In minutes she was drenched, the cotton nightgown and robe plastered to her body, the rain trickling down her cheeks. Nothing existed in the world but darkness and lightning and thunder.

Then she saw him coming to meet her.

"Idiot!" She had to shout to be heard above the surf and the thunder. "Go away. Don't you have any sens—"

His mouth was crushing hers, hot, open, moist, invading.

She groaned as she collapsed against him. "No, Andrew, this isn't—"

"Yes, it is." His hands were quick, jerky as he stripped her robe away and let it fall to the sand. "Don't lie to yourself, love. This is why you're here." His hands were warm, hard, as he cupped her breasts through the damp cotton of her gown. "Lord, you feel so good."

She arched helplessly toward him. Sweet heaven, he was right, that was why she was here. All the rest was lies.

He pushed down the clinging cotton of the bodice of the nightgown, his fingers plucking feverishly at her nipples. She bit her lower lip to keep from crying out as the muscles in her stomach clenched. Fire. Need.

Then he was pulling her toward the cliff. "This way," he muttered. "Shelter."

Shelter in this deluge? She didn't care about shelter. She only wanted him to touch her, come into her. She wanted to run her hands over the hard muscles of his back as he—

"Here." It *was* shelter—of a sort. A beach blanket was spread beneath the jutting overhang of the cliff. Andrew was stripping quickly. "Lie down, please," he said. "It will have to be quick the first time. I'm burning up."

So was Lily. She was experiencing a desire so intense and mindless, all she could do was stand there, wanting him.

He was almost nude now, his back to her, a pale, powerful shadow in the darkness.

She took a step toward him, then another. Her arms encircled his waist, her aroused nipples pressing into the flesh of his back. He felt so good. Hard, warm, sleek. "Andrew . . ."

He froze, his muscles locking. "Lord, Lily." A long shudder rippled through him, and the muscles of her stomach contracted in a silent gasp as she felt him hardening, readying. "Please. I can't—" He broke free and whirled to face her. "Quick, love." His hands urgently tugged the gown over her hips. "I have to have—" He pulled her down on the blanket, and was between her thighs. "Take me into you," he cried, then plunged deep.

Lily wasn't conscious of the primeval sound issuing from her. Hardness, heat, thickness, ruthlessly seeking into the heart of her. "Yes, oh, yes." She spoke through clenched teeth. "Please . . . more."

He was giving her more. Plunging, withdrawing, thrusting, his breath coming in harsh gasps. His hands slid around her to cup her buttocks in his warm, hard palms. "Hold me." He drew her up and forward to meet each wild, forceful stroke.

She clenched around him.

Andrew's throat arched as he threw his head back, his body tightening like a bowstring. "Lily!"

Wild, she couldn't *stand* for it to go on. The tears ran down her cheeks as she dug her nails into his tight buttocks. Dear heaven, so good . . . She couldn't *stand* for it to end.

There was no choice. The fury between them climaxed with the same explosive urgency with which it had begun.

Andrew collapsed on top of her, his elbows braced on the blanket to spare her his weight. She could feel his heartbeat thundering against her naked breasts as he fought for breath.

What had happened? she wondered dazedly. How had they come to this point, when she had never intended to give in to him?

Several minutes passed before her own breath steadied enough for her to speak. "Andrew, we have to talk."

His lips feathered her temple as he lifted off her and moved to her side. "Presently. For the moment let's just lie here and listen to the storm." He cuddled her close, his arm drawing her spoon fashion against his warm body.

"I have to get back to Cassie."

"You've only been gone a short time." His callused hand cupped her breast and squeezed gently. "Probably less than thirty minutes." His warm tongue plunged into her ear. "We were both pretty impatient, weren't we?"

Frantic, she thought. Starved for each other. She had never dreamed she could want anyone so desperately as she had wanted Andrew this night.

His thumb flicked teasingly over her left nipple. "It will be better next time. I'll be able to take more time in pleasing you."

Her nipple was hardening, a tingle starting in the center of her womanhood. Lord, she was wanting him again already. "Don't do that. I don't want to be touched any more."

His hand halted its teasing caress but remained cupping her breast. "Yes, you do," he said quietly. "You want me to touch you as much as I want to do it. You were caught off guard, and now you're panicking because you think I'm going to take advantage of your need and try to use it to dominate you."

She stiffened. "And are you?"

"No. I'm no manipulator. I want to make you happy." He paused. "I *can* make you happy, if you'll let me."

"Like this? Sex isn't everything."

"It's a start. You can't deny you need it." His teeth gently closed on her earlobe. "I can give you what you need. Use me."

Her breast was swelling beneath his hand, she realized with a feeling of helplessness. In another minute she wouldn't be able to think of anything but what her body wanted from his. "No!" Taking Andrew by surprise, she abruptly rolled away. "I don't use people. This was a mistake." Her gaze wildly searched the darkness around them. Where the devil was her nightgown? "You wouldn't let it end with sex. You'd blow it up into something more."

"I need this too," he said quietly as he sat up. "You know I've been wild to have you. I'd be satisfied for a while with just sex."

"And then?"

"When I'm not satisfied any longer, you can cut me off. In the meantime we'd have had a hell of an affair. Tempting?"

He knew it was tempting, she thought. He seemed to be able to sense and play on her emotions as Cassie did the keys of her piano. "I have to get dressed and go back to Cassie."

He knelt beside her. "Lily . . ." He stroked her wet hair back from her face. "It's all right, love. Don't be so frightened." He glanced around, spotted her nightgown, then shook his head. "You can't wear the gown. It looks like a dish rag." He picked up his sweat shirt and pulled it over her head, putting her arms in the sleeves as if she were a little girl unable to dress herself. "This is wet, too, but it's fleece-lined, and not drenched through." He settled the shirt down over her hips and onto her thighs. "I wish I could see you in it. You must look sexy as hell, with those long legs . . ." He trailed off and gave her a quick, hard kiss. "Run along. See, I'm not trying to hold you. I'm letting you go."

She jumped to her feet and turned to leave.

"Take a hot shower as soon as you get home, and be sure to dry your hair before you go to bed," Andrew said briskly. "I'll stay here and watch until I see the lights go on inside the cottage. I'll come as usual to be with you and Cassie on the beach tomorrow afternoon."

She had already ducked from beneath the rocky overhang and was walking quickly down the beach through the rain.

His soft voice followed her. "And I'll be here tomorrow night, love."

She started to run. It wasn't Andrew she was running away from, she told herself. Andrew was sitting back there, watching her leave, certainly not in hot pursuit. It was only sensible to hasten her pace to get out of the downpour.

He had said he was letting her go. Why did she feel that by doing so he had only forged new links in the bond between them?

Andrew carried a brown paper bag when he came down the trail from the cliff the next day. He called a greeting to Cassie, playing in the surf, and then plopped himself down beside Lily and placed the bag beside her.

"What's that?"

"Your nightgown and robe. I washed and dried them when I got back to the cottage."

Lily felt the color flood her cheeks. "Thank you," she said, feeling awkward. "I'll return your sweat shirt, of course."

"No hurry." Andrew smiled full at her. "You could wear it when you come to me tonight."

The top buttons of his black shirt were open, revealing the strong line of his tanned throat and the springy brown thatch that covered his chest. Her palms tingled, and she felt a sudden urge to reach out and touch him, run her fingers through that triangle of hair and— She pulled her gaze away. Good heavens, she was turning into some kind of nymphomaniac. "You're taking too much for granted."

He shook his head. "Sex like we had is addictive. We're both crazy for more." He grasped a handful of sand and slowly let it run through his fingers. "I lay in bed last night thinking about how you felt, the way you smelled, the sounds you made. Did you think about me?"

"Yes," she said, watching the sand sift through his long, slender fingers.

"And did you ache as much as I ached?"

She closed her eyes, remembering those hours she had tossed and turned the night before. "Yes."

"I want to see all of you. I'll bring a flashlight tonight."

She swallowed hard and opened her eyes. "Can we talk about something else?"

"What do you want to talk about?"

"Anything." She drew a deep breath and tried to ease the tension gripping her. "I don't really know anything about you. Do you have a family?"

He nodded. "A mother, a stepfather, and a half sister."

"Are you close?"

An affectionate smile illuminated his face. "Oh, yes."

"Where do they live?"

"Sedikhan. My stepfather, Jon, is chairman of the board of the Clanad."

"So that's how you get so much time off," she said lightly.

His smile vanished. "I do my work without shirking. There's no nepotism in the Clanad."

She had hurt him. "I didn't mean to—" She broke off in exasperation. "Well, how do you expect me to get to know you, when you practically answer me in monosyllables?"

"There's no use describing my family, when you'll be meeting them soon."

She stiffened. "You said they were in Sedikhan."

He nodded and picked up another handful of sand.

"I have no intention of taking a trip of that distance to meet your family, Andrew."

"Not right away. I know you're not ready for a commitment like that." His gaze dropped to the sand in his hand. "But perhaps you and Cassie would like to meet Gunner and Quenby. They're less than a mile away."

Lily frowned. "You mentioned them once before. Tell me about them."

"Quenby used to be my nanny before she married Gunner Nilsen. Gunner works for the Clanad, too, and has always acted as . . . well, as a sort of guardian. Would you like to meet them?"

" 'Sort of guardian.' And the Clanad is 'sort of a corporation,' and your job is 'difficult to describe.' " Lily shook her head. "You're impossibly vague."

He grinned. "Cassie told me how lack of precision annoys you. You have to have everything logical and neatly pigeonholed. Some things can't be explained, Lily. You just have to rely on your instincts."

"I don't trust instinct."

His grin faded. "I know." He shrugged. "Well, do you want to meet my friends?"

She suddenly knew she very much wanted to meet Andrew's friends. Perhaps they would cast a little light on the complexity of his personality. "Yes, I think that would be a good idea."

He threw aside the sand in his hand. "Okay, in a few days."

"Why not today?"

He smiled. "Because I think you'll feel safer coming to me at night and letting me love you if I stay a stranger for a while."

"That's crazy."

"Is it?"

No, he was right, she realized. She was not ready for emotional intimacy even though she had accepted Andrew physically. How the hell had he known that about her, when she hadn't even been aware of it herself? She experienced a frisson of uneasiness as she looked up into his calm face.

"No." She quickly glanced away from him to Cassie. "There's no hurry. I can wait to meet your friends."

"How's Cassie?" Quenby asked as soon as Andrew walked into cliff house. "And when am I going to meet her?" She gave Gunner, who was lounging in a chair in the living room, a meaningful glance as she walked toward the kitchen. "I've had nothing to do but eat, swim, and sleep since I got here. You know I can't stand to be idle."

Gunner made a face. "So she's punishing me by taking over the cooking."

"We can't all be gourmet cooks," Quenby said defensively. "And I need something to do." She paused at the door and glanced over her shoulder at Andrew. "When?"

"Soon," Andrew promised. "Probably a few days."

"Good." A teasing grin lit her face. "I thought I'd taught you not to dally, Andrew. It took you eight years to get around to meeting your child, and at this rate it will be another eight years before you introduce her to me. I might just as well have stayed in Sedikhan, where I was appreciated."

"Maybe you won't be needed here." A frown crossed Andrew's face. "Lord, I hope not, Quenby."

The grin faded from Quenby's face. "Me too. There's no sense in worrying. It could all be a tempest in a teapot." She blew him a kiss and disappeared into the kitchen.

"Maybe you'd better not wait that few days to bring Cassie and Quenby together, Andrew," Gunner said quietly.

Andrew's gaze flew to Gunner's face. "You've heard something?"

"Nothing conclusive. One of the men in Security called and said the theft of the records from Henry's office had been traced to Said Ababa."

"The institute?"

Gunner nodded. "It will take time for them to decode Henry's records, then track down Lily and Cassie. But they'll do it. I know those bastards." He smiled bitterly. "They never give up until they find what they want. I remember when they had us penned up like animals waiting for slaughter and—" He shook his head to clear it of the corrosive memories. "But that was a long time ago."

"Still, they haven't given up trying to get the Clanad back."

"Never. They've known where we were ever since

we were given sanctuary in Sedikhan, but they can't touch any of us there."

"So they decided to go a different route to get what they want."

Gunner nodded. "I'm putting a watch on Lily's cottage and the road to the highway. We may have plenty of time, but then again . . ."

Andrew felt the muscles of his stomach tighten. "Lily's not ready to come with me yet. She'd fight me."

Gunner gazed at him with silent sympathy.

Andrew's hands clenched at his sides. "I can't blow this, Gunner. It means too much to me."

"I know."

Andrew turned away, the movement heavy with weariness. "Tell Quenby that I want you both to come to the beach tomorrow to meet Lily and Cassie."

Four

It was a boldly whimsical thing to do, and not in the least like Lily. She should have had more sense than to give in to the impulse, she told herself as she hurried down the incline toward the beach. She wasn't one of the flip, aggressive college girls Andrew was surely accustomed to dealing with, and there was no way she could pull this off with panache.

Then, as Lily caught sight of Andrew standing on the moonlit beach a few yards away, she almost turned around and ran back to the cottage, like a frightened child.

"You *did* wear it for me." A delighted smile lit Andrew's face as his gaze ran over her. She was garbed only in his sweat shirt, which came to her upper thighs and left her long legs bare. "Lord, you look gorgeous."

"It was an impulse," she said quickly. "I didn't exactly wear it for you. I just thought I'd—"

"Don't spoil it."

The smile was fading from his face, and she suddenly couldn't bear it. "You said you wanted to see me in it." She tried to shrug casually. "No big deal."

"I think it's a very big deal. It's the first time you've done something just because you knew it would make me happy."

She strolled toward him. "I don't know why it should please you so much. It's certainly not the most flattering garment I've ever worn. I feel all legs."

"You are all legs. Glorious legs. Magnificent legs. Didn't I ever mention I was a leg man?" His admiring gaze lifted to her face. "I wasn't sure you'd come tonight."

"I wasn't sure either." She stopped in front of him. "I feel shy. That's probably why I wore the sweat shirt. A touch of bravado."

He held out his hand to her. "Let's see if you're capable of more than a touch, Lily."

She hesitated, and then slowly placed her hand in his and let him lead her across the beach toward the cliff. "That sounds ominous. What are you planning on doing to me?"

"Enjoying you." His clasp tightened. "Are you wearing anything beneath that sweat shirt?"

"No." They had reached the rocky overhang, and she turned to face him. "It seemed unnecessary at the time."

"Oh, it would have been." He drew her into the hollow of his hips, his palms cupping her buttocks, and he undulated against her, his bold arousal making heat tingle through her. She clutched at his shoulders as he said, "This is much more convenient." He pushed the shirt up to her waist, his hands kneading the flesh of her bottom. "Isn't it, love?"

The rough denim of his jeans felt coarse against the softness of her belly, and the studs pressed into her hips. As his long, hard fingers dug into her buttocks with just enough force to titillate but not hurt, she found herself uttering frantic little cries while she moved against him. "Andrew . . ."

"What a lovely sound." He parted her thighs, his hand cupping her womanhood, rubbing, petting, his thumb pressing, toying, rotating. "Again," he said thickly. "I want to hear it again, Lily."

Lily's knees almost gave way as sensation after sensation seared through her. "I don't . . . think I can take any more of this."

"Yes, you can. Just a little more." He took a step back and whipped the sweat shirt over her head and threw it aside. "I told you I wanted to see you. I brought a flashlight."

"There's moonlight."

"It's not enough." He pulled her into the deeper shadows formed by the rocky overhang and reached down to pick up the shiny metal flashlight on the beach blanket. "Now, stand very still, love."

A brilliant cone of light pierced the darkness. She had been expecting it but still felt a jolt of shock. The circle of light played on her face and then slowly moved down to capture her left breast. "Oh, yes. How beautiful."

Lily's heart began to pound harder, and she

could feel a burning sensation between her thighs as she stood in the darkness, chained by the golden circle of light. *Chained*, yes, the precise word. She felt helpless, unable to move except at his command. Her nipples were hardening, pointing with arousal as she felt Andrew's gaze on her. He was only a hazy shadow behind the light, yet in some crazy way she felt as if he were the light itself.

The beam moved slowly to play over her other breast.

She could hear his breathing quicken in the darkness, and found the knowledge of his arousal incredibly erotic. She took an impulsive step toward him.

"No," he said sharply. "Not yet." The light moved down to reveal the tight curls surrounding her womanhood. He took a deep breath, and when he spoke his voice was thick. "I just touched you there. My palm is still tingling from it. Soon I'll touch you there again."

She was frozen in place as he gazed at her for a long time. Why didn't he move? Speak? She couldn't breathe, she couldn't think; she could only stand there caught in a haze of heat and hunger and the hot circle of light.

The light flicked out.

She gave a low cry and flung herself at him. He met her, lifted her, frantically adjusting his clothes, and then they were joined. "Take—" The rest of her words were lost as his mouth covered hers in the same open, frantic joining.

Her legs curled around his hips as they sank to the blanket on the ground.

• • •

"I told you it would get better." Andrew buried his lips in the curve of Lily's naked shoulder. "Though we still have a long way to go. I can't seem to slow down. I guess I want you too much."

"It doesn't matter. It was beautiful." Lily's voice was low as she looked out onto the moon-dappled patchwork of the beach. She suddenly giggled. "Of course, it could be the fact that we weren't both sopping wet, with a thunderstorm threatening to overwhelm us at any second."

He went still. He reached over and flicked on the flashlight, his gaze searching her face. "You sounded as young as Cassie just then."

"Well, I'm not exactly ancient. I do have my moments of youthful exuberance."

"But you don't often let them come to the surface. You always have to be so damn sensible and mature." He paused. "And in control."

"I am sensible and mature." She sat up and once again pulled on his sweat shirt. "And anyone independent wants to be in control. I have to leave now."

"You're running away again."

"You're pushing me. You said you wouldn't push me."

He was silent.

"I told you I couldn't give you what you wanted. You wouldn't listen to me."

"You'll give me what I want. It's only a question of time." A hint of desperation threaded his voice. "But what if there's no time left?"

She frowned. "What do you mean?"

He didn't answer for a moment. "Nothing. I guess I'm just impatient. And you're so damn wary." He paused. "Talk to me. Tell me about Tait Baldor."

She froze. "I don't want to talk about him. You said you'd read the tabloids, so you know all there is to know. It's all water under the bridge."

"No, it's not. It's still with you, and I'm paying the price. You don't trust me. You buried it but you didn't let it go." He reached down and turned off the flashlight. "Now there's only me and the darkness. And I don't count. Tell me about Baldor."

"Are you trying to use some kind of amateur psychology to cleanse me of my sordid past?" she asked with biting sarcasm. "I've been through that charade, thank you. In case the newspaper missed it, perhaps I should tell you I spent six months under the care of a psychiatrist after Tait's trial."

"I know. You were close to a total breakdown. Who could blame you?"

"*I* blamed me. I blamed myself for everything. If I hadn't been so stupid, my mother would be alive today."

"She trusted Baldor, too, Lily."

"Because I loved him. She always wanted me to have a love like the one she had with my father. When she saw how crazy I was about Tait, she wanted to believe in him." She paused, struggling with the anger that was choking her. "And the son of a bitch murdered her."

Andrew was silent.

"And do you know what? When the medical

examiner stumbled on the proof during the autopsy, I wouldn't believe Tait had done it. I was so besotted with him that I let the bastard steal half a million dollars from my mother, then poison her so that he could steal whatever was left from me." She laughed harshly. "And I wouldn't believe he'd done it. I told the police it must have been someone else. They had to ram the evidence down my throat before I'd testify at Tait's trial. I was that much of a fool."

"Not a fool," Andrew said gently. "You were nineteen years old, shy and reclusive. You and your mother lived alone, and both of you tried to believe the best of everyone. You were a perfect target for a con artist like Baldor. He walked in and charmed you both until you were dizzy. You weren't stupid, only naïve." He paused. "And trusting."

"So trusting, I put my mother into her grave. So trusting, I talked her into trusting him too." She smiled bitterly. "Oh, yes, I was a great one for trusting."

"Trusting is good, Lily," Andrew said. "You made a mistake in judgment, but—"

"A mistake? Tell that to my mother. Tell her trusting is good." Her voice was vibrating with intensity. "Because I'm done with it. These days I believe what I see and what can be proved to me, not what I'm told. I'll never be used or manipulated again."

"Hence the baby by artificial insemination," Andrew said softly. "You couldn't bear to have another relationship, so you chose to go to Henry."

She nodded jerkily. "Don't you understand? I

had to have someone. I couldn't eat or sleep. I was so alone. I loved children, and I thought—" She broke off, and then continued fiercely. "I'm a good mother. I went to three doctors, and they all said I should give myself a few years before I made a decision, but I couldn't wait."

"No, I know you couldn't."

"I *needed* someone. If I'd been alone any longer I don't know if I could have survived." She stopped, and then said shakily, "Henry understood."

"Henry's a very understanding man."

"You're talking to me as soothingly as those doctors who turned me down. It was the right decision, dammit."

"I'm not arguing. It was the only decision at the time that would have assured your survival. You've made a good life for yourself and Cassie, and there's no question of your devotion to her." He reached out and covered her hand with his own. "You even ran the risk of the press's digging up that old scandal, when you allowed Cassie to go on tour."

"She deserved the chance to see if she wanted the life of the performer." She withdrew her hand from his. "Well, are you satisfied now? Do you enjoy playing father confessor?"

"Lord, no." An age-old weariness weighed in his voice. "It hurts me. It always hurts me."

"Always? You speak as if you're a priest, or something." She rose abruptly to her feet. "Well, now that you're finished with your interrogation, I believe I'll bid you good-bye."

"Lily, it was necessary. We had to get everything out in the open. I could have done it another way, but I wouldn't do that to you."

"I don't know what you're talking about, but I damn well don't like your digging into my past." Lily turned away and ducked from beneath the rocky overhang of the cliff. "Back off, Andrew."

"It had to be open and clear, so that you'd realize what happened in the past with Baldor simply cannot happen with me."

"You bet it can't."

"For God's sake, Lily, I'm no con man trying to hurt you."

"How do I know? Tait was a hell of a lot less mysterious than you. You work for a corporation located conveniently in a foreign country. You supposedly have all the time in the world at your disposal." She paused. "And, when I come to think about it, the way you've played me bears a remarkable resemblance to stalking."

"Yes, it does," Andrew admitted. "So does that mean you're going to cut me out of your life and not see me again?"

Pain shot through Lily with a force that startled her. Not see Andrew again? Andrew was youth and radiance, sexuality and sensitivity. How could she give him up? She hadn't realized until that moment how totally he had captured her, both mentally and physically. "No," she said as she started across the sand. "Why should I care why you want to see me? You said I should take what I wanted from you, and that's what I'm doing."

"Lily."

She stopped and looked over her shoulder.

"I'm bringing Quenby and Gunner to meet you tomorrow, if that's all right."

"I thought you wanted to wait a while."

"Things have changed."

She nodded jerkily. She, too, was aware that their relationship had changed in some significant manner that night. Andrew's probing had brought back too much pain, had opened wounds she had thought long since healed. And by identifying himself with her pain Andrew had drawn closer to her emotionally than he had by making love to her. She would never again remember that horrible episode with Baldor without recalling the moonlit night when she told Andrew about the pain and betrayal. He had made himself part of it and brought them to a greater level of intimacy than Lily ever would have thought possible. Had he been perceptive enough to realize that this closeness could blossom from anger and pain? The ease with which Andrew was able to read her was beginning to make her edgy.

"May I bring them tomorrow afternoon?"

"Suit yourself." Her pace quickened as she strode down the beach away from him.

"Their coloring is so similar, they might be brother and sister," Lily said as she watched Cassie playing beach ball with Quenby and Gunner Nilsen. Both Gunner and his wife were tall, blond, and possessed the type of splendid good looks prevalent in Scandinavia. It was difficult to determine their ages. If there were threads of gray in the Nilsens' hair, they were lost in the white-gold fairness. Both of them were running around shouting and hurling that enormous red ball with a vigor and youthfulness that made them appear little older than Cassie. "Are they both Swedish?"

Andrew shook his head as he lifted a cup of coffee to his lips. "Quenby's of Swedish descent, but Gunner isn't Scandinavian at all. He's from Garvania."

Lily frowned. "Garvania? I never heard of it."

Andrew shrugged. "It doesn't exist anymore. Garvania was annexed by Said Ababa over twenty years ago."

Lily's brows cleared. "Well, at least I've heard of Said Ababa. That's the totalitarian country that's always having border disputes with Sedikhan and Tamrovia. Right?"

"Right."

Lily's gaze returned to the trio playing a short distance away. "Your friends are nice people," she said sincerely. "And they've certainly charmed Cassie. I've never seen her take to anyone but you this quickly."

"It's not surprising. Quenby says Gunner never grew up. He's probably enjoying Cassie as much as she is him. And Quenby's always been a sucker for kids."

"Does she have any children of her own?"

Andrew nodded. "A son attending the University of Marasef, in Sedikhan. Jed's a nice kid."

"How patronizing you sound. He can't be that much younger than you."

Andrew's hand clenched on the Styrofoam cup. "Are you trying to relegate me to the campus set again? I thought we'd gotten past that obstacle. Why are you putting barriers between us?"

"There are already barriers between us."

"It's strange you never notice them when I'm making love to you," Andrew said softly. "They just disappear then, don't they?"

Lily could feel the warm color stain her cheeks. "Sex is a very basic pleasure and tends to make one forget everything . . . for an hour or so."

"Making love."

"What?"

"What we do isn't sex, it's making love." Andrew lifted the cup to his lips and drained the coffee in two swallows. "Someday you'll understand that."

She gazed at him, startled. "I don't know—"

"Yes, you do." His hand crushed the cup with sudden violence. "You do care about me, dammit. You just won't admit it." He jumped to his feet and tossed the crushed cup aside. "I'm going down to play ball with Cassie."

Lily watched him stride away from her and resisted the impulse to call him back. What was the matter with Andrew this afternoon? There was something brooding and violent about him; she had sensed those dark emotions in him the moment he had appeared on the beach with Gunner and Quenby two hours before.

"May I join you?" Gunner asked. "I must be getting more decrepit than I thought. Your daughter really put me through a workout."

"You don't look worn out."

Gunner dropped down beside her. "I'm a fantastic actor. Do you think I'd let that little kid know the older generation can't keep up with her? Now, though, I'm ready to let Andrew take the punishment for a while. Is there any coffee left?"

Lily poured him a cup from the thermos and held it out to him. "Black?"

He nodded as he took the cup. "I'll have to make you some real coffee some time." He sipped the hot liquid gingerly. "I prefer it with cinnamon and ginger."

"How exotic. Is that how they drink it in Sedikhan?"

He nodded. "Exotic is only how you perceive it. Once you get used to anything it becomes homey and comfortable." He looked down into the depths of his coffee. "Sedikhan is a good place to live. You'd like it there."

Lily stiffened. "Would I?"

"Quenby does. It took her a little while to get used to it, but she wouldn't live anyplace else now."

"I'm glad she has a happy life there."

Gunner sipped his coffee. "So am I. My job is in Sedikhan, and I'd hate to have to leave it."

Lily turned to look at him. "Would you really give up your career for her?"

"Of course. I couldn't be happy if Quenby weren't happy."

"You must have an extraordinary relationship," Lily said thoughtfully.

"Quenby is an extraordinary woman." Gunner's face softened as his gaze traveled to his wife. "She's warm, loving, honest, and absolutely reliable."

"I can see how she must have been a wonderful nanny for Andrew. Cassie's already crazy about her."

He nodded. "As I said, she's extraordinary." His gaze shifted to Lily's face. "And so is Andrew."

"Henry said he was remarkable." Lily made a face. "But he's certainly evasive. I don't even know what he does for a living. He says he fixes things."

Gunner smiled. "He certainly does."

"But he has so much time off."

"Actually, every day since he's been here he's worked all morning at that small hospital down the coast. Andrew usually tries to help out wherever he can, and heaven knows there are enough people who need him. Didn't he tell you?"

"Hospital?" She frowned. "No, he didn't."

"I'm not surprised. Andrew doesn't talk about his work."

Lily threw up her hands. "Now you're being as mysterious as Andrew. I'm beginning to think you're both CIA or something."

Gunner laughed in genuine amusement. "I guarantee you're wrong on that score. Neither one of us has anything to do with an undercover agency." His smile faded. "However, Andrew's work can be very dangerous on occasion, and he needs all the support we can offer him."

A chill gripped Lily. "What kind of danger are you talking about?"

"I shouldn't be talking to you at all." He drained his cup. "It's Andrew's place to tell you about his work." He met her gaze directly. "But I'd like to say that there are a great many people who have put their lives and more than their lives into Andrew's hands, and he's never failed them."

"More than their lives?"

He nodded gravely. "Trust him, Lily. He cares a great deal for you."

"Did he ask you to speak to me?"

"Andrew fights his own battles." He grinned. "And now I have to pry my wife away from your daughter and take her home before she decides to kidnap Cassie. Just look at them together."

Lily's gaze went to Quenby Nilsen, whose face was illuminated with joy and affection as she laughed at Cassie. "I hope you and Quenby will come again soon," she said impulsively. "I work in the mornings, but most afternoons we come down to the beach."

"We'd like that," Gunner said. "Andrew's been keeping the two of you to himself for far too long." He lifted his hand in farewell as he started across the beach toward Andrew, Quenby, and Cassie.

Their lovemaking that night was wild, erotic, and nearly brutal in its intensity.

Andrew couldn't seem to get enough of her, and Lily found herself responding on an equally primitive level. They came together time after time, until exhaustion finally overtook them and they could only lay clinging to each other, breathing in short, harsh gasps.

"Why?" she asked when she'd gained enough breath to speak. "Something's . . . different."

He didn't look at her as he rolled away from her and began to dress. "Did I hurt you?"

"No." She slowly sat up. "Did you mean to hurt me?"

"No!" He turned to look at her in horror. "Lord, no, I'd never want to hurt you. I *couldn't* hurt you." His lips twisted in a mirthless smile. "I suppose you don't believe me, after what just happened."

"I wasn't exactly fighting you. I think . . . I . . . I liked it. I was only curious. It seemed out of character, and you were upset with me this afternoon."

"That doesn't mean I'd become violent."

"But you don't deny—"

"I wasn't angry. I was frustrated." He located her nightgown and handed it to her. "I'm still frustrated, dammit. You won't see what we have together, and we're running out of time."

She froze. "You have to go away?" She moistened her lips with her tongue. "I don't know why I'm surprised. I knew you couldn't stay forever." She pulled the nightgown over her head and settled its cotton folds around her hips. "After all, you have a job to return to, and Cassie and I will be going back to San Francisco in a few weeks anyway. Maybe it's just as well that—"

"It's not just as well," Andrew interrupted with barely controlled violence. "Stop backing away from me, dammit. Face what we have together. It's not sex alone that draws us to each other, and it's not Cassie alone either."

Lily hurriedly stood up. "I have to leave."

"Listen to me, Lily." Andrew's face was set and stern in the moonlight as he rose to his feet. "Time has been against us from the very beginning. I can't let it keep separating us." He kicked the beach rug at his feet. "Lord, I haven't even slept in a real bed with you. We've never sat down at a table for a meal or done any of the intimate, commonplace things men and women do together.

I go back to the cottage and see Gunner and Quenby together and I want what they have so badly that it twists inside me and makes me—" He broke off and drew a deep breath. "It's been too long. I can't take it any more. *Tell* me what the hell you feel for me."

"I don't know. Do we have to talk about this?"

"Yes," he said flatly. "I know you want me. I know you like me. What else do you feel? Do you think about me all the time when you're not with me? Do you want to protect and cherish me? Because that's the way I feel about you."

Lily could feel the tears sting her eyes. "Andrew, I don't want to hurt you."

"Then don't hurt me. Tell me you care for me. I know damn well you could if you'd lower those barriers and believe I'm not a bastard like Baldor." His voice became a whisper of urgent persuasion. "You don't have to give me your complete trust now. Just give me a little today and then a tiny bit more tomorrow and then a little more the day after that." He smiled with an effort. "Maybe in a couple of decades we'll finally get there."

Sweet Mary, he looked so unhappy. She had never meant to hurt Andrew, yet there was no question she had done so. Pain swept through her, and she took an impulsive step forward. "Andrew, I *want* to trust you."

"Well, that's a start, anyway."

She took another step and was in his arms, pressing her tear-wet cheek to his chest. "I don't want you to go away," she said. "It would hurt me if you left me."

His arms tightened around her. "Another giant step," he said thickly. "Since I've already established that I don't want to hurt you, I guess I'll just have to stick around a while longer."

Joy exploded within her. "But you said you'd run out of time. I don't want to interfere with—"

His lips moving on her own were hard, sweet, hot. "Interfere. Lord, sweetheart, interfere!"

She broke free from him and took a step back. "I'm . . . I'm not promising anything." She was almost stammering, she realized in disgust. "You must do as you think best."

"You're shying away again." A radiant smile lit his face. "But we've definitely made a breakthrough, my love."

She smiled back at him, feeling young, exhilarated, and brimming with hope. Great heavens, how long had it been since she had felt like this? "I believe we have at that, my lo—" She stopped.

He nodded understandingly. "One day at a time. A little today, a little more tomorrow. You can do it, Lily."

"Yes." Standing there, with her gaze lingering on the strength and gentleness of his face, she could almost believe the formula could work, that Andrew could make it work. "Maybe I *can* do it, Andrew."

Five

She had heard something.

Lily fought her way from the depths of sleep to half waking. The sound in the living room had not been loud, but it should not have existed. Cassie? Maybe Cassie was ill or had gone to the bathroom.

The whisper of sound came again, now just outside her bedroom door.

"Cassie?" she called, struggling up on one elbow. "Are you all right, baby?"

No answer. The sound had stopped.

Perhaps she had only imagined the noise, she thought drowsily. She started to settle back on her pillows. Then her eyes flew open as she went rigid with fear. She had called out, and the sound had stopped. Someone knew she was awake and was trying not to arouse her suspicions.

The sound had been a footstep!

A burglary? How had a thief gotten inside the

cottage? She was sure she had locked the front door when she had come back to the house that night. Sweet heaven, why was she worrying about the *how*'s and *why*'s? There was someone just outside her bedroom door!

She rolled over in bed and carefully pulled open the drawer of the bedside table, her ears straining to hear any trace of sound outside the door. Nothing. But someone was still there. She could *feel* it.

She took the pistol out of the drawer, slid off the safety lock, and swung her feet to the floor.

The footsteps started again.

Lily froze, her hand clutching the butt of the pistol. She would wait until the thief came into her room, and then—

But he was not coming toward her room. The sound of the steps was fading as he moved away from her door.

He was going toward Cassie's room.

No! She was out of bed and halfway across the room in the instant of realization. She threw open the door and flicked on the wall switch.

"Get the hell away from her, damn you!"

The man who whirled away from Cassie's door was a little over medium height, dark-complexioned, with a scar slashing down his right cheek. Ugliness. Not only of the body, but of the soul. The impression of malice overwhelmed Lily even as his startled gaze fell on the pistol in her hand. "You don't understand." His words were thickly accented. "Put down the pistol."

"The hell I will. Get away from that door and sit

down over there." She gestured with the pistol to the high-backed easy chair across the room. "We'll see what the sheriff says about this little burglary." She stepped from the doorway of the bedroom in the direction of the telephone on the pine end table by the couch. "I understand the authorities are very hard on thieves and vandals in beach communities. You may go away for a long—"

Pain!

Her head exploded into shards of agony.

"The child. Get the child," said a guttural voice behind her. Pain again, this time in her right temple.

Darkness.

From where she lay on the floor Lily could see the door of Cassie's room thrown open wide, the rumpled covers of the bed, the door of the closet ajar. Cassie. She had to find Cassie.

Cassie was gone.

Lily turned her head, and a bolt of agony made her blind and dizzy. Her stomach heaved with nausea, and she lay very still, trying to get the strength to make a new effort. Why had they taken Cassie?

She forced her eyes open and saw the gun on the floor beside her. She reached out, her palm closing on the butt of the pistol. Why hadn't they taken the gun? Didn't they know she would go after them? She couldn't let them take her little girl.

She struggled to her knees and then waited for

a fresh wave of pain to pass. The next attempt put her on her feet.

The telephone. She had to call the sheriff.

She staggered the few feet to the table and picked up the receiver. Dead. The phone was dead. They must have cut the wires.

She wished she could think. She lifted her hand to rub her temple, and it came away wet. Blood. She gazed at it curiously before wiping her fingers absently on the skirt of her nightgown. What could she do now? She didn't even know how long they had been gone or how long she had been unconscious. They might be a hundred miles away and traveling farther with every passing second. She was too weak to try to walk the ten miles to town to get the sheriff. She had to find someone to help her.

Andrew.

But he had said their cottage was a half mile from the crest of the cliff, and the trail up to the summit would be at least another quarter mile. She couldn't make it.

Cassie.

Of course she could make it, dammit. She moved carefully toward the front door, keeping her neck very straight, so that the pain was only a throbbing ache. She had to make it to Andrew. She was *going* to make it.

The cool breeze on her cheeks felt invigorating, but it didn't help the nausea. Well, that would have to go away too. She would not have it. She wouldn't be beaten by those hoodlums. She held tightly to the banister as she made her way slowly down the steps of the deck.

Why didn't they answer the door?

She pounded again, but the thump sounded weak and ineffectual even to her own ears. She was so tired, but she had to pound harder or they wouldn't hear. She lifted her hand again.

A slit of light appeared beneath the door. They had heard her. The door swung open.

Andrew.

His fair hair was tousled, his eyes glittering in the lamplight. Why didn't he say anything? He was looking at her so strangely.

Maybe she was the one who was supposed to say something. Her lips tried to form words, but nothing came out.

"What is it, Andrew?" It was Quenby's voice, issuing from somewhere in the room behind Andrew.

Finally one word struggled from her lips. "Cassie . . ."

She pitched forward in a dead faint.

Andrew was sitting in the chair beside the bed when Lily opened her eyes. His hand instantly covered her own on the counterpane. "It's going to be all right. We'll get Cassie back, Lily."

Light poured through the bay window across the room, revealing an unfamiliar bedroom. Of course, it was the cliff cottage, she realized. She had come to Andrew for help. "What time is it?"

"Almost eight o'clock. You showed up on the doorstep at three in the morning, and you've been unconscious ever since." A muscle jumped in his cheek. "You scared the hell out of me. You were covered with blood, and you looked as if—"

"They hit me. Twice." Lily tried to sit up. "I thought there was only one man, but the other must have been standing beside the doorway when I—"

"You don't have to go into the details." He pushed her back against the pillows. "What's important is getting you well and getting Cassie back."

"Have you called the sheriff? They should put out an all-points bulletin."

"Not yet."

She looked at him incredulously. "Why not? You've had five hours. Those horrible men have *Cassie.*"

"Don't get so upset. It's not good for you." Andrew frowned with concern. "Quenby has training as a nurse and says she doesn't think it's more than a mild concussion, but you should take it easy and—"

"Don't get upset?" Lily sat bolt upright in bed, ignoring the jolt of pain in her temple the movement caused her. "My daughter has been kidnapped by . . ." She trailed off as she lifted her hand wearily to her head. "I don't know who they were. I don't even know why they took her. I thought they were burglars, but one of them said . . . For some reason they wanted Cassie. Ransom? For God's sake, do they think I'd live in a cheap bungalow like that if I had any money? And what if it wasn't ransom?" Panic iced through her. "What if they hurt her, Andrew? What if—"

"They won't hurt her, love. I promise you."

"How can you promise anything?" Lily swung her feet to the floor. "I have to call the sheriff. I saw one of the men. I can give them a description. That should help them to find him. Maybe I can look at some mug shots and identify—"

"These men wouldn't be in the mug books, Lily."

"They could be. You don't know if—" She broke off as she caught sight of his expression. "Dear God," she whispered. "You do know." She couldn't comprehend it. Andrew *knew* these men. He knew something about Cassie's disappearance. It was all a part of this nightmare from which there was no awakening. She gazed at him in horror. "You did this?"

"No." Andrew's voice was sharp. "Do you think I'm a monster? I wanted to kill when I saw you standing on the doorstep last night."

"Then you know who did it," Lily said flatly. "You know who took Cassie."

"Yes." Andrew's lips twisted. "So perhaps I am to blame. I wasn't absolutely sure they were tracking you and Cassie, so I took a chance on waiting to see if I could persuade you to come with me willingly."

"A con instead of a blackjack?" Lily asked coldly. "You might have succeeded. You certainly showed a talent for the game." She shook her head incredulously. "I was actually beginning to believe in you."

"Lily, everything I told you was the truth."

"Your confederates are going to be disappointed when they find out I'm not a pigeon worth plucking." She laughed harshly. "You should have kept in closer touch with them, and they wouldn't have expended such needless effort. I can see how the newspaper publicity might have made it appear Cassie was the goose who laid a stockpile of golden eggs, but—"

"This isn't about money, Lily."

"What do you mean? Of course it's about money. What else could it be?"

Andrew leaned wearily back in his chair. "It's about Cassie. And about me."

"What are you saying?"

"There won't be a ransom note."

She gazed at him in silence. "You said you wouldn't try to take her away from me, you bastard."

"I won't. I didn't. These are *not* my confederates, dammit. They don't want Cassie because they think they might get money from you. They want her because they know she's my child."

"That's absurd. They couldn't know. Henry wouldn't talk to a stranger."

"Henry didn't have to tell them. A month ago his office was broken into and his files were stolen. They were in code, but we knew a cryptologist could probably break it, given enough time. Henry notified us at once, but it was too late to detect any traces by the time our team reached the university."

"Wait a minute." Lily held up her hand. "Why were his records in code?"

"They are . . . were confidential."

"Of course, but that seems a little extreme."

Andrew was silent.

"And why were they particularly interested in your daughter? Are you a Wall Street tycoon or something? Maybe a member of the millionaire-boys club?"

Andrew flinched. "Lily, I know this is difficult for you, but—"

"Well, are you?"

"I have enough money to be comfortable. Money is easy to come by in the Clanad. We don't need much in Sedikhan." He paused. "But I told you this isn't about money. I won't receive a ransom note either."

"Then, by all that's holy, what is it about?"

Andrew shook his head. "You wouldn't understand, and if you did, you wouldn't believe me." He smiled crookedly. "Hell, you wouldn't believe me if I told you the sun rises in the east, at the moment."

"I'd certainly question it. Tell me anyway."

"No, there'll be time enough for that later. Instead, I'll tell you Cassie is safe and that those men have no intention of physically harming her. She may be frightened, but that's the extent of the damage they'll do to her while she remains here in the U.S."

"While they're here? Are they planning to take her out of the country? Where, for heaven's sake?"

"Said Ababa."

She shook her head dazedly. "What the hell is happening here?"

Andrew impulsively put out a hand as if to touch her. As she flinched back, his hand dropped to the arm of the chair. "She won't be hurt." His hand closed on the arm of the chair, his knuckles white. "I know you can't believe in me, but please believe that, Lily. For your own sake, believe Cassie's safe."

"How can I, when you won't tell me anything? Not even where she is or—"

"I don't know where she is." Andrew's eyes were haunted. "I'm expecting a phone call from Gunner at any time, with more information. He and Quenby are trying to track them."

"Track? This isn't the day of the Pony Express or Buffalo Bill. Call the FBI, dammit."

"We can't." Andrew paused. "It would be dangerous for Cassie. These agents don't want the reason they took Cassie to come to light, and a public investigation would do that. Besides, Gunner has a better chance of tracking them. The Clanad has agents in this area, and this is Gunner's job."

"His specialty is finding kidnapped children? What kind of a job is that?" She closed her eyes. "I want my little girl back, damn you. I don't care about your Clanad or those bastards who took her. I just want Cassie home."

"We'll bring her home. Safe."

Her eyes opened wide and glittered coldly as she gazed at him. "I don't know what kind of mess you've involved yourself in, but Cassie and I aren't part of it. If Cassie is hurt because of you, I'll punish you, Andrew."

"Oh, I know you will," he said thickly. "You already have." He smiled with an effort. "Gunner thinks they haven't had time to smuggle her out of the country yet. They don't have a network in this—"

The phone rang in the other room.

Andrew pushed back the chair and jumped to his feet. "That must be Gunner. I'll be right back."

Lily heard him pick up the phone and answer, but she couldn't hear what he was saying. She struggled to her feet, swayed as a wave of dizziness assaulted her, then moved slowly across the room. Clinging to the jamb of the door, she was just in time to see Andrew hang up the receiver. "Does he know where she is?"

"Oh, for Lord's sake." Andrew gazed at her in exasperation. "You look as if you're about to collapse any minute. Did you have to follow me?" He didn't wait for an answer, but covered the distance between them in three strides, lifted her in his arms, and carried her back to the bed. "And yes, he knows where they are. The agents who took Cassie are Hamid Kalom—he's the one with the scar—and Said Baharas. They've taken Cassie to a lodge called the Eidelweiss Inn, about a hundred miles north of here. The inn is owned by a Said Ababa national, and Gunner says they're waiting for a plane to arrive at the private airport nearby to take Cassie out of the country." He placed her on the bed. "Cassie is being held in one of the chalet bungalows on the grounds of the lodge and she's fine, Lily."

"How could she be fine, when she's probably

scared to death? And if Gunner and the men he's with know where Cassie is, why don't they go in and get her? Suppose the plane they're waiting for arrives and they take her away?"

"Lily, these agents aren't . . ." Andrew halted, searching for words before he finished. "Professional."

"What do you mean?"

"The government of Said Ababa has always relied on brute force to get what it wants. The men who run that country are acquirers, not creators. You can see how slapdash this entire operation is turning out to be. No planning."

"Then let's take advantage of their blundering and get Cassie back."

"We will," Andrew said quietly. "But we have to go slowly. Gunner says that the first reaction these agents will have if cornered is violence. Kalom particularly has a reputation for viciousness. They'll strike out and won't care that what they're destroying has value to them."

"Cassie," Lily whispered. "They'll hurt Cassie."

"No harm will come to Cassie. I'll just have to be careful to make sure Cassie's protected before Gunner moves in."

"And how do you propose to do that?"

"I'll find a way. I'm leaving for the inn immediately. Gunner is sending a helicopter to pick me up."

"I'm going with you."

Andrew nodded. "I thought you'd say that. I suppose I can't convince you to stay here and let us handle it?"

"No."

"Or that after the bang on your head you shouldn't do anything but rest?"

"No."

"All right." Andrew held up his hand as she started to speak. "But there are conditions."

"Conditions! My daughter is—"

"You do what I tell you to do." Steel edged Andrew's voice. "No questions, no arguments."

"And if I don't?"

"Then you don't go with me."

"I could follow you to this Eidelweiss place."

"And if you did, I'd use any method at my disposal to make you do as I said. There'd be no option then."

All trace of boyishness had vanished from Andrew's demeanor, and the hard-edged toughness of which Lily had caught only fleeting glimpses had come to the surface. "I could lie to you." She paused. "As you lied to me."

"I never lied to you."

"The hell you didn't. You came here and conned me while persuading Cassie you were the greatest thing since sliced bread, and all for some purpose of your own."

"I didn't con—" He stopped, and then broke out with violence, "Lord, you don't even know what conning is. I could have shown you. I could have—" He halted again and then shook his head wearily. "There's no use trying to convince you while you're so worried about Cassie. Will you give me your word you'll let me lead, if I take you?"

She gazed at him, frowning. "Okay," she said

slowly. "But if I think you're moving too slowly I may change my mind and go my own way."

He smiled crookedly. "Why doesn't that surprise me?" He turned to leave the room. "I'll go down to your cottage and pack your bag and get a few things for Cassie. Should I bring anything in particular?"

"No, anything will— Wait, there is something. Her music box." Lily felt the tears sting her eyes. "It's a little-girl pianist sitting at a baby-grand piano that revolves and plays a Bach prelude. I bought it for her when she was only three, and she takes it with her everywhere she goes. She plays it every night before she goes to sleep, and . . ." She stopped and tried to steady her voice. "It should be on the nightstand beside her bed."

"I'll get it." He glanced back over his shoulder. "Will you keep still and rest? I'll help you get to the bathroom to clean up and brush your teeth when I get back."

"I'll lie here." Lily closed her eyes. "And I'll let you help me. I'm not about to waste my strength on a useless gesture of independence, when I may need it later to help Cassie."

"Very sensible. I hope to hell you continue in that vein."

She heard Andrew's retreating footsteps, then the closing of the door.

He was gone. She was alone. The knowledge sent a surge of depression through her that she knew was completely unreasonable. Except for Cassie, she had been alone for many years, and this was no different. The closeness she believed to have been forged between her and Andrew she now considered a mirage that had vanished. She had to accept the fact. Thank heaven she hadn't fallen completely under his spell. Yet if she hadn't come perilously close, then why was the hurt of his betrayal such a throbbing wound?

Good heavens, she was worrying about a relationship that had scarcely started to bud, when she should have been thinking only of Cassie. In her mind Andrew and Cassie seemed bound together, and she was having trouble isolating one from the other. Andrew had given her Cassie, and now because of him Cassie had been taken away. What horrible mess had Lily become involved in when she had walked into Henry's office nine years earlier? Stolen files, kidnappings, international intrigues centered around Cassie?

No, it wasn't Cassie who was the center of the plot; it was Andrew. He had said Cassie had been taken because she was his daughter, so that meant he would be walking into greater danger than Cassie faced.

She would *not* worry about him. Andrew was an adult, and no doubt responsible for this episode. Cassie, on the other hand, was the innocent victim. Poor baby. Those thugs probably terrified her. The scar-faced man had looked like something out of a horror—

Lily's eyes suddenly flew open. How had Andrew known what the man had looked like? Or, for that matter, what had taken place at the cottage at all?

She had fallen unconscious before she had been able to tell him anything.

Yet Andrew had mentioned the scar-faced man she had *seen*, and Gunner had taken off on the kidnappers' trail before she had regained consciousness.

Madness. Everything was madness. So many questions, and Andrew would answer none of them.

"Why would a Middle-Eastern national name his hotel Eidelweiss?" Lily asked as the helicopter sluggishly began its descent in the center of a small glade.

Andrew shrugged. "Why not? Said Ababa hasn't gained a squeaky-clean reputation on the world scene, and what's better than an alpine image? The Said Ababans are seldom original. As I said, they prefer to acquire what someone else has created or developed." He nodded at a figure standing on the perimeter of the woods. "There's Gunner."

"Why isn't he watching the bungalow where they're keeping Cassie?" Lily's hands clenched the arms of the seat. "What if they take her away while—"

"Gunner will have left a watch," Andrew interrupted. "He knows his job."

The helicopter settled on the ground, and Gunner started toward them.

The young pilot cut the engine and turned toward Andrew. "Will you need me for the return trip?"

Andrew shook his head. "No return, Jake."

Lily's gaze flew to Andrew's face. "What do you

mean? When we get Cassie we'll need a way to return to the cottage."

Andrew opened the heavy metal door. "No return," he repeated as he jumped down from the helicopter and turned to lift Lily to the grass beside him. "It's too late to go back. We can only go forward now."

"Cryptic nonsense," she said succinctly. "It may be too late for you, but Cassie and I will certainly go back."

Andrew took their two small suitcases from the cockpit and closed the door, waving the pilot away. "We'll see. It's not the time to talk about it now." He picked up the suitcases. "Let's find out if Gunner has any new information."

She was immediately distracted, and turned and hurried to Gunner. "Cassie, is she well?"

He nodded, his gaze raking her face. "You look like death." He turned to Andrew. "You couldn't keep her from coming?"

"Not without putting her in a straitjacket and locking her in a dungeon." Andrew shrugged. "And even then she'd probably have found a way to follow me. I thought it would be better to have her under surveillance."

Gunner nodded. "Quenby said that Lily wouldn't stay behind."

"Where is Quenby?" Andrew asked.

"We've rented a bungalow at a hotel near the one where they're holding Cassie. Quenby's waiting for us there." Gunner took Lily's elbow and urged her toward the woods. "Come on. I have a rental car parked a few hundred yards on the other side of the woods. Let's get you to it before you collapse."

"I'm all right," Lily said impatiently as they entered the woods. "When are we going to be able to free Cassie?"

"Soon. I didn't want to move on this one without Andrew's sanction. Cassie is his daughter, and he has the right—"

"Cassie is *my* daughter," Lily said fiercely. "I raised her, I'm the one who cared for her when she was sick and shared—"

"No one's disputing your right to her," Gunner interrupted. "That's why you're here." He paused. "But you may not be able to help her, in this case. She may need Andrew."

"Why?" Andrew asked sharply. "You said she was all right."

"Physically, she's fine," Gunner said. "They haven't touched her, but naturally all this has been a shock to her. She saw Lily lying on the floor and thought she had been murdered."

"Of course it's been a shock," Lily said. "For heaven's sake, she's been kidnapped."

"And she's very sensitive." Gunner met Andrew's gaze. "More sensitive than I first thought. We may have a problem."

"Lord," Andrew whispered. "That's all we need right now."

"What kind of problem?" Lily asked. "What's wrong with Cassie?"

They had reached a gleaming dark blue Buick, and Gunner opened the rear door of the car. "I'm jumping the gun. It's too early to tell if there's even a problem. We'll worry about her mental state once we have her away from these jokers."

"And when will that be?"

"Tonight," Gunner said. "If Andrew thinks Cassie can take it."

"Cassie's tough." Andrew said, frowning. "I never thought she'd react this way."

Lily got into the back seat of the car. "It's my decision, not Andrew's. We go after Cassie tonight."

"No, Lily." The softness of Andrew's voice failed to hide its steely determination. "The operation goes forward when I say so, and not before. I won't rush in and risk tearing Cassie to pieces. I'll make a decision after I've studied the situation this afternoon."

Before she could speak he slammed the door, went around to the front of the car, and climbed into the passenger seat beside Gunner.

Six

"He won't talk to me," Lily said in despair as she plopped herself down in the chair across the dining table from Quenby. "Andrew just sits in that damn bedroom staring out the window at the chalet where they're keeping Cassie. I want to *do* something."

Quenby smiled sympathetically as she poured coffee into Lily's cup. "I know how you feel, but believe me, Andrew is doing something."

"Thinking." Lily shook her head. "That's not enough. We have to help Cassie. I can't bear . . ." Her voice broke. "I can't stand this, Quenby. I don't understand it. It doesn't make any sense."

"You won't have to wait much longer. Andrew's very good at what he does."

"And just what does Andrew do so well?" Lily asked with a mirthless smile. "Is he a spy or a mysterious troubleshooter like Gunner? He's certainly never confided in me about his past—or his present either, for that matter."

"He would if he could," Quenby said gently. "He's never wanted to keep anything from you. Andrew has always been afraid you couldn't accept him for what he is."

"It might help if I knew what that entailed." Lily looked into the depths of her coffee. "Or maybe it wouldn't. It's too late now."

"Don't say that." Quenby's expression was troubled. "The situation is too complicated for you to make decisions, when you don't have all the facts."

"Then give them to me."

"I wish I could. It's not my—"

"You needn't give Quenby the third degree." Andrew stood in the doorway of the bedroom. "You'll know everything soon enough." He turned to Quenby. "Where's Gunner?"

"He went to the lodge to see about getting a waiter's uniform. Do you need him? I can go get him."

Andrew shook his head. "Just so we move fast. I want to get Cassie out of there right away."

"At last we agree," Lily said.

"It won't damage her?" Quenby asked hesitantly.

Andrew's lips tightened. "I doubt if she'll even know we're there."

"Oh, my Lord," Quenby whispered.

"What are you saying?" Lily asked, gazing from Quenby's horrified expression to Andrew's stern one. "How can you know any—" She stopped, trying to gain control. "This isn't fair. I need to know."

Andrew nodded. "I know it's not fair, but Cassie will be all right. I promise you, Lily!"

"And I'm supposed to believe you? I don't want to have to rely on anyone's word. I want to help. I want to go with you."

Andrew shook his head. "They'd recognize you, and that would endanger Cassie. Gunner can handle it."

"Gunner's only one man." Lily turned to Quenby. "Aren't you afraid for Gunner?"

"Not against only two men." Quenby smiled. "It took me a long time to accept Gunner's vocation, but I've finally come to terms with it."

"But these are violent men." Lily raised her hand to her cut, bruised temple. "Gunner should have help."

"I'll be along," Andrew said quietly. "Did you think I'd let him go alone?"

Fear sleeted through Lily. "No!"

"You want to go yourself but you'd deny me the pleasure?" Andrew smiled sadly. "Perhaps you don't resent me as much as you think you do."

"I don't want anyone hurt."

"I assure you Gunner won't let me do anything interesting. He's very selfish when it comes to adventures like this. I'll just go along to run interference with Cassie. She may need someone to block . . ." Andrew's voice trailed off. "Gunner is planning to take them when they call room service for dinner."

Quenby nodded. "He has someone in the kitchen waiting for the call. They phoned for lunch at three, so it will probably be eight or nine before they order dinner."

"So we wait," Andrew said wearily. "Will you tell Gunner when he comes back that I'll need a uniform too?"

Quenby nodded. "He's probably already arranged to get you one. You're going to rest?"

"I have to try to relax. Cassie can't stay like this. We have to bring her back right away." Andrew turned and went back to the bedroom and closed the door.

"I don't want him to go without me," Lily whispered.

Quenby smiled. "He'll be safe with Gunner."

Lily gazed at Quenby in helpless silence.

"Why don't you admit to yourself that you care for him," Quenby said gently. "It would make it so much easier for you."

"I don't love him. I don't love anyone but Cassie."

"Then why are you all tied up in knots at the thought of anything happening to him?" Quenby reached over and covered Lily's hand with her own. "Listen, Andrew is very special, and he's worth loving, dammit. I don't know anyone who gives more to others than he does. He deserves to get something for himself, for once."

"I told him I couldn't give him what he wants."

"I think you'll change your mind." Quenby's clasp tightened affectionately. "You're not as tough as you pretend, and there will come a time when you'll want to be able to reach out and help Andrew." Her expression clouded. "If you can. Heaven knows, we've all tried to help him. He's so damned alone."

"We're all alone."

"Within ourselves, maybe. But sometimes something wonderful happens." Quenby's face was suddenly glowing. "Someone special comes along and the loneliness goes away. And when that happens you're a fool if you don't reach out and grab it, then hold on tight." She sat down and leaned back in her chair. "And you're no fool, Lily."

Lily's gaze went to the doorway of the bedroom. "I don't know. I thought I was a fool to trust him. Now you say I'm a fool if I don't."

"What do your instincts tell you to do?"

The faintest smile touched Lily's lips. "Not you too? Andrew's very big on instincts. I'm afraid I can't afford to trust my own. I don't have a very good track record, and the consequences are too high when they fail you."

"Lily, you can't—" Quenby stopped as she saw Lily's expression become guarded. "You're wrong, but you'll have to learn that for yourself." She reached for the carafe of coffee. "Let me refill your cup. You're going to need the caffeine. I think it's going to be a long night."

"Andrew?" Lily knocked softly and then opened the door to the bedroom. "Are you awake? It's eight o'clock. Gunner says Kalom should be calling for room service soon, and it's time for you to dress."

There was no answer from the bed across the room.

"Andrew?" Her hand fumbled for the light switch on the wall beside the door.

"Don't turn on the light."

Andrew's voice came from the direction of the leaded casement windows across the room. Silhouetted against the glass his dark shadow suddenly reminded Lily of those first days when she had known him only as a mystery figure on the cliff. Not that he was any less mysterious now, she thought ruefully. "Gunner says there's still a little time, but he thought we should alert you. He's brought you one of those Tyrolean-style uniforms the waiters wear." She tried to smile. "You should see him. With his fair hair he really looks the part."

"I'll get dressed in a minute. Come in and close the door."

She opened her lips to protest and then closed them without speaking. There was something terribly lonely about that lean silhouette framed against the window. She took a step forward and closed the door. "Did you sleep? Quenby seems worried about your getting rest. I guess that's the nanny syndrome."

"I slept. I can usually force myself to sleep when it's necessary."

"Good. For someone so easygoing Quenby was positively fretting. She and Gunner really care about you."

"Does it surprise you that I can occasionally inspire affection in others?"

"Of course not. I knew you could be very charming when you—"

"I've been standing here thinking about you."

"You should be thinking about Cassie."

"You're part of her and she's part of you. One leads to the other." He paused. "I've been thinking about you and your mother."

She stiffened. "I don't want to talk about my mother."

"I know. It still hurts you. It's natural that it should, but not that the wound should still be so raw. I've been trying to puzzle it out. Tell me, do you think your mother would blame you for making the mistake of trusting Baldor?"

"Who wouldn't blame me?"

"Lily, did she love you?"

"Yes . . ." Lily's voice thickened. "Yes, she loved me."

"Then don't you think she would have forgiven you for being fooled by Baldor?"

"Yes, but I—"

"Then why can't you forgive yourself?"

"This isn't about forgiveness."

"I think it is. I think that's why the wound hasn't healed all these years. You were bitterly sorry, but it was too late for you to tell her, to ask to be forgiven. You *needed* to ask someone for forgiveness, and there was no one there."

He was right, she realized with astonishment. Until he had put it into words, she hadn't known how desperate had been that need.

"Are you sorry, Lily?" he asked gently.

"Of course I'm sorry."

"There, you've said it now. Your mother would have forgiven you for your mistake, so let it go,

Lily. Forgive yourself and be as happy as she would have wanted you to be."

Something incredible was happening inside her; something cold and tight was loosening, warming. "She was . . . my best friend."

"Then don't condemn the memories of your best friend to live side by side with bitterness. She deserves better than that."

Lily closed her eyes. "I'll think about what you've said."

"There's one more thing I wanted to say to you."

"I said I'd think—"

"I love you."

The words came out of the darkness with stunning force.

Her eyes flew open. "You never cease to surprise me."

"I wanted you to know. I've been afraid to use the word *love* before, but now it doesn't matter if it scares you off. The situation couldn't be any worse than it is." His hand clenched on the drapes. "Things are going to happen tonight that you won't understand, things that you may hate." He paused. "Lord, I hope you won't hate me too."

"I don't hate you." Her emotions were in such turmoil, she wasn't sure what she was feeling for him at that moment. "I don't think I could hate you. Though heaven knows I wanted to cut your throat when I found out you knew something about Cassie's kidnapping."

"But you won't let yourself love me, either." His tone was strained. "You may never love me. I've known that all along, but I had to try. Since the moment I saw you I knew there would never be anyone else for me."

"That was only a few weeks ago. Hardly enough time for a permanent—"

"A few weeks?" He shook his head. "It's been over eleven years since I saw you the first time."

She stiffened, gazing at him in bewilderment. "You *saw* me?"

He nodded. "Henry had requested I come to Franklin University to help with one of his patients, and I saw you walking across the campus. I just stood there, looking at you, and I thought: Here it is. This is mine."

Lily swallowed to ease the sudden tightness in her throat. "How impossibly romantic. Just what I would expect of you."

"I didn't feel romantic. I felt"—he paused—"as if everything had come right, as if all the parts of the puzzle had come together, letting me see the entire picture for the first time." His tone became bittersweet. "And what a picture it was. I was just a kid whom you wouldn't have looked twice at even if you hadn't been undergoing the fallout from that nightmare with Baldor. Everything was against us: time, circumstances, my work. So I had to take the only chance that would assure me a place in your life."

"Cassie."

"Cassie." Andrew straightened his shoulders as if shifting a burden. "I just thought you should know." His hand released the drapes, and he turned away from the window. "Will you ask Gunner to come in now? We'll have to make a few plans while I dress."

"A few plans? You can't expect to walk in and overpower those men without a struggle."

He turned on the lamp on the table beside the bed. "Don't worry—it will be over in a matter of a few minutes once we're in the room. We just have to be sure that neither man is near Cassie when Gunner attacks."

She shook her head. "You're making it sound too easy. These are vicious men, Andrew."

His lips tightened as his gaze went to her cut and bruised temple. "I know. They hurt you. I didn't think I believed in revenge, but I was wrong. I'll see that they suffer for it, Lily."

"I don't want anyone to suffer. I just want Cassie safe." She turned and opened the door. "And then I want answers to a few hundred questions."

"You'll get those answers," Andrew said quietly. "But you probably won't like what you hear."

"I should have gone along." Lily paced the length of the room. "Andrew said it would only take a few minutes, and—"

"It's only been fifteen minutes," Quenby said soothingly. "I'm sure they'll be back soon. There's truly very little danger, Lily."

"How can you say that? Those men hit me over the head and kidnapped a helpless little girl."

"Gunner will take care of them. He's handled men far more dangerous than they." Quenby hesitated. "It should be over by now. Do you want to go see what's holding them up?"

Lily stopped short. "Could we? There would be no danger to Cassie?"

Quenby got to her feet. "We can at least walk over toward the chalet and see if there's any sign of—"

The door opened, and Gunner walked into the room.

Lily whirled to face him. "Cassie?" Her gaze searched eagerly over his shoulder. Andrew wasn't with him. Her heart lurched sickeningly. "What's happened to Andrew?"

"They're both still at the chalet," Gunner said. "She's not hurt, Lily. Andrew will bring her as soon as he finishes working with her."

"Working with her?" Lily ran toward the door. "You're not telling me the truth. Something's happened to her."

"No." Gunner stepped in front of the door and grasped Lily's shoulders. "Andrew will fix it. You don't want to go there now."

"The hell I don't." Lily tore herself from his hold and ran out the door and down the path toward the chalet next door. The lights were streaming from the casement windows, and the chalet looked as innocent and cozy as a gingerbread house. What had happened to Cassie in that house? She threw open the front door. "Andrew? Where's Cassie?" She entered the foyer. "I have to see Cas—"

Two men were lying crumpled on the floor of the living room.

Lily froze, staring down at them. She recognized the scar-faced man at once as the intruder in the cottage. The other man was heavier, older. . . .

They were dead, she thought with sick horror. They had to be dead. No one could be alive and still be so rigidly inert. And their faces . . . features contorted with pain, mouths open in a silent scream, eyes glassy and staring straight ahead.

"You shouldn't be here." Andrew stood in the doorway across the room. "Dammit, I told Gunner to keep you away."

"They're dead," she whispered.

Andrew shook his head. "They're only locked."

"But they look . . ." She tore her gaze away from the pain-racked bodies on the floor. "I want to see Cassie. What's happened to her? Did they hurt her?"

"No, they didn't hurt her." Andrew hesitated. "It would be better if you'd go away and leave me with her for a while longer. I may be able to—"

"How can I leave her?" Lily strode toward him across the room. "I have to see her." She pushed past him into the bedroom. "Cassie, I'm here. Are you—Oh, my God."

Cassie was lying on the bed, still dressed in the pajamas she'd worn the night before when Lily had tucked her into bed at the cottage. Her apparel was the only hint of similarity between that child and the effigy lying before her. A waxlike pallor clung to Cassie's face; her eyes were wide open and unseeing, her muscles locked in the same deathlike rigor as those of the men in the living room.

"Cassie?" Lily whispered as she moved slowly across the room toward the bed. "Baby?"

Cassie didn't answer. Her gaze remained unflinchingly fixed straight ahead.

Lily sat down on the edge of the bed, unaware of the tears rolling down her cheeks. She brushed a lock of sandy hair gently back from Cassie's temple. "Answer me, love."

Cassie showed no reaction.

"What have they done to her?" Lily asked dazedly.

"Nothing." Andrew was standing beside her, his hand clasped comfortingly on her shoulder. "She's done it to herself, Lily. She's withdrawn inside and locked everything out."

"Locked. You said that about those men out there."

"It's not the same," Andrew said gently. "There's no pain where she is. It's as if she's sleeping."

"Comatose."

"A little like that."

"Why?" Lily asked brokenly. "How could this happen?"

"Shock. She loves you more than anything in the world, and she saw you lying on the floor hurt and bleeding. She called to you, and you didn't answer. She thought you were dead. There was too much violence, too much horror, and she had to shut it out." Andrew's hand moved to rest gently on Lily's head. "But it's not permanent. I can bring her out of it."

"You?" Lily shook her head violently. "We have to get her to a hospital. She needs medicine, doctors."

"It wouldn't help. She wouldn't respond. They wouldn't know how to help her."

"And you would?"

"I'm the only one who could know," Andrew said quietly. "We're alike. I can reach her. I hoped I'd be able to wake her before you had to see her, but she's very stubborn."

Lily's hands tightened on Cassie's blanket. "I know you mean well, but can't you see that Cassie has to have professional help? Look at her."

Andrew nodded. "Cassie will have professional help, Lily. This is what I do. This is my job."

"You're a doctor?"

He smiled. "No, but I fix things that are broken. The way Cassie is broken." He gently pulled Lily to her feet. "Now we have to get Cassie out of here and back to the cabin. Gunner and his men will be here soon to pick up Kalom and Baharas."

"What will they do with them?"

"Put them on a plane for Sedikhan. Gunner has a jet standing by at a private airport near here."

"You said the Clanad was more efficient," Lily said abstractedly, her gaze moving yearningly over Cassie's face. "Sweet heaven, I don't know what to do. This is all so crazy."

"Then trust me. You know I care about Cassie and would never hurt her. I *can* fix what's wrong with her. Just this once, trust me, Lily."

She gazed up at him and was caught by the sheer intensity of his plea. He believed what he was saying. He believed he could help Cassie. Why not let him try? "What do we do first?"

Relief brightened the gravity of his expression.

"You've already started." He bent and lifted Cassie in his arms. "You've given me your confidence. That's always the most important step. Now let me do the rest. We'll take her back to our cabin, and I'll get to work."

He turned and carried Cassie toward the open door.

Andrew placed Cassie carefully on the bed and turned to Lily and Quenby. "I need one more thing from you, Lily. Leave me alone to do my job."

"Why can't I stay?"

"You wouldn't understand, and you'd undoubtedly be upset." Andrew smiled crookedly. "I can usually close everyone out, but I wouldn't be able to do that with you. My concentration would be blown."

"Why do you have to concentrate? You're not performing brain surgery, for Pete's sake." She ran her fingers nervously through her hair. "Or maybe you are. How the devil do I know?"

"Come with me, Lily." Quenby put her arm around Lily's shoulders. "It will be better if we wait in the living room. Andrew will call us when Cassie wakes up."

If she woke up.

No, Lily wouldn't even consider the possibility that Cassie wouldn't be all right. She let Quenby propel her toward the door. "How long?"

"As long as it takes." Andrew was no longer looking at Lily, but at Cassie. He dragged a chair close to the bed and sat down on the cushioned seat. "You can turn out the light. I won't need it."

Quenby switched off the light as she drew Lily from the room and closed the door.

"Why am I letting him do this?" Lily asked as she dropped down on the couch in the living room. "For all I know he's one of those acupuncture specialists and he's going to stick pins into Cassie."

"You're doing it because you believe more in instinct than you think you do," Quenby said gently. "Just as you believe in Andrew."

"What's he doing to her?" Lily asked, her gaze meeting Quenby's. "For heaven's sake, tell me. I deserve to know. How would you feel if it were Jed who was lying in there?"

Quenby sat down in a chair opposite the couch. "Terrible. I thank God every night my son's never gone into this kind of shock. Gunner and I were lucky. Jed isn't nearly as sensitive as most half-breeds. Gunner says it's due to my very pragmatic genes."

"Half-breed?" Lily gazed at her in bewilderment.

"Gunner is Clanad and I'm not."

"What difference does that make? The Clanad is a corporation, not a . . ." Lily stopped and sat up straighter. "What are you telling me?"

"The truth," Quenby said. "Or as much of the truth as I think you can take right now. I've decided we're all being ridiculous. Gunner thinks it's Andrew's place to tell you, and Andrew doesn't want you frightened any more than you are already." She made a face. "It's typical muddled male thinking, and I've been going along with it.

In the meantime, you're suffering more from confusion than you would be from facing the facts."

"And what are the facts?"

"That Andrew is not sticking pins into Cassie but is still performing in-depth surgery. He's cutting through the barriers and splicing and knitting up the raveled ends. He's healing her." Quenby paused. "Telepathically."

Lily gazed at her in stunned disbelief. "I beg your pardon?"

"I know. I know." Quenby pulled a face. "Now you think we're all a bunch of escapees from the cracker factory."

"The thought did occur to me." Lily started to get up from the couch. "I think I'll just go in and tell Andrew I've changed my mind."

"Don't do that." Quenby said, her tone suddenly urgent. "Interrupting him now could be dangerous for Cassie. He knows what he's doing."

Lily sat back down. "You're telling me Andrew is a telepath?" she asked carefully. "You're either joking, in which case you chose a lousy time for it, or you're demented. I don't believe in telepathy."

"Then you'd better start," Quenby said simply. "Andrew is a telepath, and so is Gunner. My son, Jed, also has certain telepathic powers." She paused. "And so does Cassie."

"No!" Lily shook her head violently. "Now I know you're crazy. Don't you think I'd know if my own daughter were a telepath?"

Quenby shook her head. "Cassie's talent is latent. She probably shows flashes of intuitiveness, but without training she might never reach full potential."

"And what is her potential?" Lily asked caustically.

"It's different for everyone. Perhaps her telepathic ability will remain submerged by her other talents all her life. Perhaps later it will dominate." Quenby shrugged. "Personally, I'm hoping Jed's telepathy remains latent. Having powers like Andrew's can be a curse, not a blessing."

"I can't believe I'm sitting here listening to you."

"You're listening because those instincts you're so skeptical about have been sending out signals since the moment Andrew appeared in your life."

Lily's fingers dug into the cushions of the couch. "You're saying Andrew has been reading my mind since the moment I met him?"

"Absolutely not," Quenby said instantly. "Andrew has a very strong code of honor. He would not invade anyone's privacy. Only under extreme conditions would he go underneath without your consent. But he can't help knowing things about you, picking up vibrations or feelings. With Cassie, the bond's even stronger. She has the same powers, and therefore sends actual thoughts to Andrew and receives them from him."

His name is Andrew, Cassie had said.

Someone must have called his name.

Andrew brought back the music.

Lily fought back the avalanche of memories. Coincidence, she thought desperately. It had to be coincidence.

"It's not coincidence, Lily."

Lily's gaze flew to Quenby's face in horror.

Quenby laughed and shook her head. "No, I'm not telepathic. Just an educated guess. I felt the same way when Gunner told me about his telepathic powers." She wrinkled her nose. "However, he doesn't have quite as strict a code as Andrew, and provided a demonstration that startled the heck out of me."

"What did he—" Lily broke off. "Now I'm the one who's crazy. I was actually starting to believe you."

"You'll believe me," Quenby said confidently. "It will take time to sink in, but then you'll start remembering things and putting the pieces together. I'm not going to overload you with information right now. I think you have enough to deal with."

Lily shook her head dazedly. Quenby Nilsen appeared so down-to-earth and practical. It seemed impossible that she would spout this nonsensical voodoo. "You mean there's more?"

"We've just uncovered the tip of the iceberg." Quenby leaned back in her chair. "But you've actually taken the little bit I've given you quite well."

"Because I've heard it's better to humor nut cases."

Quenby chuckled. "I assure you I'm not violent." She suddenly sobered. "There's one more thing you should know about Andrew right now. He's not blundering blindly with Cassie. He's been doing this kind of work since he was a small boy."

"Telepathic healing? You'll forgive me if I find that concept impossible to accept."

Quenby shook her head. "He can't work miracles. He can only go underneath and reinforce the will to live, he also can teach—he can straighten out most of the snarls and tangles the human mind makes for itself." Quenby added simply, "He can bring light into darkness. But to do it he has to go down and live in that darkness, feel the pain and the torment. That's what he's doing with Cassie now."

Light into darkness. "That sounds like pretty much of a miracle to me," Lily said wearily. "And too far-fetched for me to accept."

"Then why are you still sitting here? Why aren't you marching in and snatching Cassie away from Andrew? It's because down deep you want to believe in Andrew."

"I don't believe any of this," Lily said quickly. "And I certainly have no faith Andrew will be able to—" She broke off, and her head turned toward the closed bedroom door. "What's that? I thought I heard—"

Music! The silver cascade of notes from Cassie's music box.

"It's the Bach," Lily whispered. "He's playing Cassie's music box." She jumped to her feet and ran toward the door.

"Lily, he may not be ready for—"

Lily threw open the door. The lights were still out, with the room still in darkness.

The melody of the Bach prelude wove silvery ribbons of beauty through the shadows.

Cassie laughed in the darkness.

"Turn on the lights, Lily," Andrew said.

Lily's hand trembled as she fumbled for the light switch on the wall.

Cassie was sitting up on the bed. "Hi, Mom. Can I have a cheeseburger? I'm starved."

"It . . . could be arranged." Lily scanned Cassie's face hungrily. Bright eyes, good color, she was blessedly, wonderfully normal. Lily's knees felt rubbery as she walked across the room toward the bed. "How do you feel, baby?"

"Great." Cassie looked at her in surprise. "Why shouldn't I feel great? You're the one who got knocked on the head." For an instant a shadow crossed Cassie's face. "I thought those creeps had killed you. I called and called, but you wouldn't wake up. You okay?"

"Perfectly okay." Lily sat down on the side of the bed. "But I'd be even better if I had a hug."

Cassie got up on her knees and enveloped Lily in a fierce bear hug. "Andrew said you were fine. He said it over and over. . . ."

Yet Lily had heard no voice in the bedroom. No sounds had come from the room at all until the melody of the music box.

"Andrew is quite right. I never felt better than at this moment." She glanced over Cassie's head at Andrew. "I think I owe you—" She broke off, stiffening in shock.

Andrew looked ten years older. The skin was pulled tight over his cheekbones, the flesh beneath his eyes imprinted with ink-black shadows. "Are you all right?"

He smiled at her. "A little tired." He stood up, his movements jerky and uncoordinated. "I think

I'll go get some air and then find somewhere to crash for a while."

"A tough one?" Quenby asked from the doorway.

Andrew nodded as he moved toward the door. "Lord, she's stubborn. She wouldn't be budged."

"Andrew!" Cassie pulled away from Lily, a touch of panic crossing her face. "Don't go. I'll be alone again."

Andrew turned to look at her. "You forgot what I told you." A smile lit his face, momentarily banishing the haggardness. "You'll never be alone again. I'll always be there when you want me."

The anxiety left Cassie's face, and she nestled back against Lily. "That's nice to know."

Lily tried to smother the twinge of hurt she felt as her arms tightened around Cassie.

"It's not the same, Lily." Andrew said, his gaze shifting to Lily's face. "I haven't taken her from you."

"Haven't you? I'm not so petty that I'd begrudge you Cassie's affection, after what you've done to help her." She smiled crookedly. "Though God knows how you did it."

"I told you how he did it," Quenby said.

Andrew stiffened. "You shouldn't have done that, Quenby. She's had enough to—"

"For Pete's sake, she's not made of glass," Quenby interrupted. "And she'll need time to assimilate it."

"Maybe." Andrew's hand rubbed wearily at the muscles at the nape of his neck. "I can't judge. I'm not thinking clearly at the moment." He turned to go.

"Andrew," Lily called impulsively.

He glanced back over his shoulder.

"Why did you play the music box?"

"Bach."

"What?"

"She identifies Bach very closely with you. You have character traits that remind her of his music. I thought it would be a comfort to her."

Lily's eyes widened. "How did you know that? Did Cassie tell you?"

Andrew gazed at her a moment without speaking. "Why don't you ask Cassie?"

He turned and left the room, with Quenby following close behind.

Seven

"He's sad."

Lily turned back to look at Cassie. The child's brow was wrinkled in a frown of concern as she gazed at the doorway through which Andrew had disappeared. "He's sad about you." Her gaze shifted back to Lily's face. "He's hurting, but you can help him."

"Right now I'm more concerned about helping you to a cheeseburger," Lily said lightly as she gave Cassie another hug and then released her. "Andrew appears to be tough enough to handle his own problems."

"He *is* tough, but he still needs people to like him." Cassie's gaze searched Lily's face. "You're afraid of him."

"Nonsense. I'm not afraid of any man."

"You're afraid of Andrew. Why?"

"I'm not—" Lily stopped. She wasn't being truthful with either herself or Cassie, and their relationship had always been founded on honesty. "He knows too much. I guess it makes me uneasy."

"But what he knows is really neat," Cassie protested. "He makes me feel"—she hesitated—"like the music. He *understands* the music, Mom."

"Cassie . . ." Lily reached up and tucked a strand of sandy hair behind Cassie's left ear as she tried to form the question she needed to ask. "You were sick, and Andrew helped you get well. How did—"

"I wasn't sick," Cassie interrupted. "I was just hiding out. Then Andrew came in and made me realize what a jerk I was being."

"And how did he do that?"

"I don't know," Cassie said, puzzled. "He was just there. At first, I couldn't hear him but I could feel him. He was kind of warm and cozy. You know, like drinking hot chocolate after being out on a cold, rainy day. Then the music came, and after that I heard him talking to me."

"And you weren't afraid?"

"Of Andrew?" Cassie looked at her in astonishment. "Andrew brought me the music. I couldn't hear it before he came, and it was getting darker and colder and very scary."

A chill went through Lily. Where would that darkness have led if Andrew hadn't forced Cassie out of her hiding place? "Quenby says it's telepathy."

"Is it?" Cassie was unimpressed. "No wonder you were a little freaked out. Don't worry, Mom, it's nothing like those stupid movies you see about telepathy. Like I said, it's kind of cozy." She swung her feet to the floor, got off the bed, and looked at the door on the far side of the bed. "I have to go to the bathroom. Is that it?"

Lily nodded as she rose to her feet. "I'll order you a cheeseburger from room service."

"With potato chips." Cassie grinned over her shoulder with impish humor. "And no vegetables."

Lily chuckled. In this bewildering world of kidnappings, foreign agents, and telepathy there were some things that never changed, thank heavens. "I'll settle for a dill pickle on the side."

"Done."

Cassie disappeared into the bathroom.

Lily's smile faded as the door closed behind her daughter. Cassie was definitely back to her old self, but that didn't mean the threat to her was over. Why had Cassie, who had always been blessedly emotionally stable, gone into shock in the first place? And why did those men so desperately want Cassie and Andrew?

Cassie had accepted the idea that Andrew was a telepath, but could Lily? The evidence seemed irrefutable, but it went against the grain for her to believe anything so outlandish. Yet, in some mysterious fashion, Andrew had brought Cassie back to her, and she felt passionately grateful no matter how the act had been accomplished.

There was no doubt she would have to think long and hard about what had transpired in the last twenty-four hours, and some decisions would have to be made. But any soul-searching could wait until Cassie had gone to sleep that night. Just now Lily wanted only to enjoy having Cassie safe and well again. She sat down on the bed, picked up the receiver of the phone, and dialed room service for Cassie's cheeseburger.

• • • •

"Where's Andrew?" Lily asked Quenby as soon as she walked into the living room the next morning.

Quenby looked up from the newspaper she was reading. "He went to the airport with Gunner to check out the condition of Hamid Kalom and Baharas before they're flown to Sedikhan. He should be back soon." Quenby's frown was troubled. "Kalom is still in bad shape."

"Bad shape?" Lily shivered. "I thought they were both dead. What happened to them?"

"Gunner," Quenby said simply. "He's not usually so ruthless, but he likes Cassie. He was mad as hell, and Andrew sanctioned it."

"Sanctioned what?"

"Pain. They're locked in pain. They'll stay that way until the lock is lifted."

"Gunner can do that?" Lily grimaced. "That's not telepathy; that's mind control."

"Some of the stronger telepaths of the Clanad are capable of mind control, but it's strictly forbidden." Quenby paused. "Except for someone like Gunner, who acts as a policeman, or Andrew, who uses it to heal."

"But you said Andrew sanctioned their pain."

"He was angry," Quenby repeated. "I've never seen Andrew so angry as when he knew how they'd hurt you. He had second thoughts this morning, and went out to the airport to remove the lock before the plane took off." She wrinkled her nose. "My Gunner isn't nearly as tenderhearted. He thought they should suffer at least until they reached Sedikhan."

"Mind control," Lily repeated, dismayed. "I thought I'd come to terms with what you told me last night, but this is different."

"Just another outcropping of the iceberg."

"The Titanic sank because of one of those outcroppings. I can already feel the water pouring into my boiler decks."

Quenby chuckled. "I guarantee that you won't sink. We'll just have to keep the influx to a minimum until you have time to repair your hull. How's Cassie?"

"Fine. Still sleeping." Lily shook her head in wonder. "It's as if all this had never happened to her. She's neither worried nor afraid."

"Andrew." Quenby smiled. "I told you he knew his job."

"I need to talk to him."

"He thought you would. He said—"

Andrew opened the door and walked into the room. He stopped short, stiffening with wariness as he caught sight of Lily. His greeting sounded curiously formal. "Hello. Did you sleep well?"

He still looked tired, Lily thought, but that terrible haggardness was gone. "Well enough. Cassie's still sleeping."

"Good. She needs it."

"How did it go?" Quenby asked.

"Rotten. Baharas is okay, but there's no response at all from Kalom."

"Well, don't worry. They'll take care of him at the compound." Quenby moved quickly toward the front door. "I think I'll go for a walk in the garden. Did Gunner come back with you?"

Andrew nodded, his gaze still on Lily's face. "He's at the lodge. He wanted to clean up some loose ends before we left."

"Then I'll go find him and make him buy me a cup of coffee." The door closed behind Quenby.

Her departure left the room echoing with a strained silence, which Lily hurried to fill. "Would those loose ends have anything to do with this telepathy business?"

Andrew nodded. "A few memory erasures to cover what happened here."

"You speak of it so casually." Lily crossed her arms across her chest to still their trembling. "Just a few erasures. And Quenby is so damn matter-of-fact too."

"We live with it every day."

Lily laughed shakily. "Gunner said the exotic becomes commonplace when you've grown accustomed to it. I don't think I'm that adaptable."

"At least you're not rejecting the concept."

"I can't. I was here. I saw those men. I talked to Cassie." She met his gaze. "As outrageous as I find the idea, I have to accept the fact that you and Gunner are telepaths. Believe me, I wrestled for a long time with that particular bogeyman last night." She straightened her shoulders. "Okay, you're telepaths. Now I have a few questions."

"Only a few?"

"First, why did those men want Cassie?" She held up her hand as he started to speak. "Oh, I know you said they wanted her because she was your daughter, but why?"

"They wanted to study her," Andrew said. "They

wanted to run tests and do some brain scans on her to see what makes her tick."

"Why?"

"Because she's the first quarter-breed the Clanad's ever produced, and they thought it possible she could be controlled and directed as they wished."

"Wait a minute. Quarter-breed? Quenby was saying something about half-breeds and the Clanad. Just what is the Clanad? It's no corporation, right?"

"Well, we do maintain several corporations." Andrew shrugged. "The Clanad actually refers to a group of refugees who escaped from Said Ababa a good many years ago. They were Garvanians who had submitted to chemical injections to induce mind expansion right before Said Ababa invaded their country. The chemical was derived from a rare plant found only in Garvania that became extinct shortly after the experiments began. This irritated the Said Ababans no end, and when Garvania was defeated, the group was transferred to a place called the Institute in Said Ababa and forced to undergo certain tests." Andrew's lips tightened grimly. "Everyone in the group was treated very harshly. My mother told me my own father's heart was fatally weakened by the treatment he received at the Institute, and Gunner has horror stories that don't bear repeating."

"And they were going to take Cassie there?" Lily whispered.

"She would have been safe until she reached the Institute." Andrew added bitterly. "They wouldn't think of damaging the laboratory animals."

"And they want you for the same reason?"

"They realized the original members of the Clanad were too strong for them to touch, but they thought the strength might have been diluted in the second and third generations."

"And is it?"

"No, but the younger generations have a greater sensitivity, which makes unskilled tampering very dangerous." He paused. "Cassie couldn't have survived the Institute, Lily. She would have locked herself away as she did last night, and been dead in a few days."

"Dead?" Lily's eyes widened in horror. "She was in that much danger?"

"It's only a matter of time after the mind shuts down before the bodily functions follow."

"You didn't tell me."

"I knew I could bring her back, and it would only have terrified you."

"Yes." She was terrified now at the mere thought of how close Cassie had come. "Quenby said half-breeds were prone to this kind of trauma. It's like a time bomb. It could have happened any time." Her voice rose in panic. "It could happen tomorrow."

"Easy," Andrew said quietly. "It took a gigantic shock to send her into a tailspin."

"And what if it had happened before?" Lily asked fiercely. "What if you hadn't been on the scene?"

"I would have been notified. You don't think the Clanad would let one of its own go wandering around without being monitored. We *care* about one another, Lily. The Clanad wouldn't let my daughter suffer."

"Just one big happy family." Her hands tightened into fists. "Well, I don't know anything about this Clanad of yours, but—"

"The Clanad isn't only mine; it's Cassie's." Andrew smiled faintly. "And you belong to it now too."

"No!"

He nodded. "A rather perilous honor, I agree. The only place where we're safe is Sedikhan, because we're under the protection of the reigning sheik, Alex Ben Raschid. Anywhere else in the world, discovery of what and who we are means we're fair game."

"Even here in America?"

"There are witch hunts everywhere. What was your reaction when Quenby told you?"

"Revulsion," she said honestly. "Fear."

"Exactly." He smiled sadly. "And you're an intelligent, civilized woman, who knows I care very much for her. There are a hell of a lot of people who are on the lower end of the scale whose reaction would be a good deal more violent. I was almost murdered when I was a child younger than Cassie, by someone who discovered what the Clanad was."

"Murdered." She swallowed to try to ease a sudden queasiness in her stomach. "They'd murder a child?"

"As you told Cassie, there are lots of weirdos running around."

Death. Andrew could have died, and she never would have known him. He never would have grown up, never given her Cassie. She dried her suddenly moist palms on the denim of her shorts. "I don't understand how anyone could—" She stopped as a thought occurred to her. "This insemination business. Was that the Clanad's way to spread its powers?"

He nodded. "We were encouraged to be donors, but it wasn't mandatory. Each parent was investigated for genetic and mental stability, and the children were monitored from birth for any sign of acute sensitivity." He grimaced. "I wanted no part of it. Until I saw you."

She laughed shakily. "Well, your investigation went off the track when it came to me. I'd just committed the most incredibly stupid act in the history of the human race, and I was on the verge of a breakdown."

"But you were a survivor, and struggling damn hard to come back to life. You're very strong, Lily. You'd have been chosen by the Clanad even if I hadn't wanted you to belong to me."

She repeated his words: "A perilous honor. When you consider you gave me a daughter who can go into shock and die at any moment."

He flinched, and she felt a stab of remorse. The words had tumbled out unthinkingly, born of bewilderment and frustration. "I didn't mean—"

He interrupted quietly. "No, you have every right to resent it. Our scientists thought the sensitivity would have vanished by the third generation, but you had no choice, and no information on which to base a decision. My only defense is that I thought I was giving you sufficient gifts to balance the bad points. Be fair: If you had the decision to make today, would you choose not to have Cassie?"

Refuse Cassie, with her sunny nature and loving heart? "No," Lily said instantly. "I'd do it again in a minute."

Andrew smiled. "Thank God."

"But that doesn't mean I hold you any the less culpable for not coming to me and telling me what I'd gotten myself into by bearing Cassie." She walked over to the chair and sat down. "Still, later is better than not at all. Let's get down to brass tacks. How can we keep this from happening to Cassie again? I assume this Institute will be sending other agents after Cassie when they find out you've have disposed of those two."

He looked at her in surprise. "I told you that you were a survivor." He smiled and nodded. "Gunner said they were an obstinate bunch at the Institute."

"Then Cassie's still in danger." Lily's hands tightened on the arms of her chair. "It hasn't ended yet?"

"No."

"Well, don't just stand there. Tell me how we're going to protect her."

"I was waiting for you to tell me." Andrew moved across the room to stand before her. "I think you've already figured it out, haven't you?"

"You told the pilot of the helicopter we could never go back, only go forward."

"Yes."

"You meant that the old life wouldn't be safe for Cassie."

"Yes."

She drew a deep breath and lifted her gaze to

his. "You meant Cassie would have to go to Sedikhan."

He nodded. "You'll both have to go. The Institute has no qualms about taking hostages, Lily."

"Of course I'd go. Do you think I'd let Cassie go alone?" Lily asked fiercely. "That is, if I decide she should go."

Andrew was silent, waiting.

"Suppose she doesn't like it there."

"She'll like it. She'll feel more at home than she ever has in her life," Andrew said gently. "And, given time with her, I can build a mind barrier that will lessen the danger of the shock factor."

"You're sure?"

"I'm sure."

Several minutes passed before Lily spoke again. "What about her music?"

"She can perform in Marasef, if she likes, but I think you'll find she's leaning more toward composition. We have excellent teachers in the compound."

"Compound?"

"The Clanad lives in a compound outside Marasef."

"Oh." She grimaced. "It sounds like a military stockade."

Andrew shook his head. "It's very pleasant. I have a house you can use until you're given one of your own. It's located only a few miles from my mother and stepfather's home. I think you'll like my mother. She and Jon are in Marasef right now, but she'll probably rush back to meet Cassie."

"She's Cassie's grandmother," Lily said softly. "Cassie has a grandmother. I never thought . . ." She trailed off.

"Is it me?" Andrew asked. "If I'm the reason you're holding back, then tell me and let me see if I can work it out."

"You seduced me."

"I did."

"Did you . . . It wasn't telepathy?"

"Lord, no! I'd never go under against your will."

A tiny smile tugged at her lips. "I think you must have done that the night Cassie was kidnapped. How else would you have known what happened, when I was unconscious and couldn't tell you?"

To her surprise, Andrew flushed. "That was an emergency. We had to know what was wrong. I'll never do it again without permission."

"So the seduction wasn't paranormal." She made a face. "I suppose I was looking for an excuse. I don't like admitting to weakness and stupidity."

"You have an excuse, if you'd only admit it."

"That I care for you?" She gazed squarely at him. "I don't know what I feel for you any longer, Andrew. It's as if I've been on an emotional roller-coaster ride for the past twenty-four hours. I've been angry, hurt, worried, afraid."

"But now the roller-coaster cars have come back to the starting gate." Andrew smiled. "And you can sit still and analyze what's happened to you. If you've gone through all this and still don't hate me, don't you think that's a good sign?"

"Maybe." She shook her head wearily. "I just don't know."

"But you'll let yourself find out?"

She stood up and started toward the bedroom

where Cassie was sleeping. "We'll see what happens when we get to Sedikhan."

Andrew went still. "You're going?"

Lily nodded as she opened the door. "Cassie and I will try it. If we don't like it, you'll have to find another solution. Okay?"

"Okay." Relief and exhilaration turned Andrew's tone buoyant. "You will like it, Lily."

She frowned over her shoulder. "None of this voodoo stuff. Promise?"

"Promise." Andrew's eyes were twinkling as he said gravely, "Absolutely no hocus pocus."

"I'll wake Cassie and start to pack. When do we leave?"

"The Clanad is sending another Lear jet to the airport tonight. It's due to arrive here about seven."

She glanced back over her shoulder. "What would you have done if I'd refused to go?"

Andrew hesitated, his smile fading. "Convinced you. One way or the other, you would have had to go. It's not safe for you here."

She had already decided that was the course he would have chosen, and she appreciated the honesty of his answer. "Then you'd have had your hands damn full," she said lightly. "It's lucky for both our sakes that I agreed, isn't it?"

The door of the bedroom shut firmly behind her.

"And I thought a compound sounded military?" Lily asked incredulously, her gaze traveling from the emerald-and-white marble tile of the foyer, to the amber-and-crystal chandelier, to the graceful black marble fountain in the adjoining sunroom, where Cassie was playfully running her fingers through a flow of sparkling water. "All the houses I've seen look like mini-palaces, and the parks are botanical gardens."

"We live here," Andrew said simply. "The compound is our home. We have very clever landscape artists and architects, and we work out trades in service in our particular specialties."

"Is there a piano?" Cassie asked.

Andrew nodded. "In the music room. I'll have Muggins take you to see it." He pressed a button on the wall beside the light switch. "But don't get too engrossed. Muggins will have a fit if you miss lunch."

"Who's Muggins?" Lily asked.

Andrew grimaced. "Mrs. Muggins was a birthday gift from my sister, Mariana, last year. She thought I needed looking after, and came up with Muggins. You mustn't let her bully you. If she goes too far just tell her to knock it off."

"I hope I can discourage Mrs. Muggins without being that rude," Lily said, shocked. "Why should I—"

"Ah, there you are, Mr. Andrew." A melodious female voice with a thick Irish brogue suddenly boomed from the room to the right of the foyer. "You're looking tired again. Are you sure you've been getting your proper rest? Sure, and the minute you're out of my sight you're into mischief again." Mrs. Muggins glided into view. "Oh, you've brought company. What a treat."

Cassie started to laugh, and clapped her hands in delight.

Lily could only stare at Mrs. Muggins in blank astonishment.

"Now, don't be rude, lad." Mrs. Muggins glided forward. "Introduce me to your guests."

Andrew sighed. "Lily and Cassie Deslin. This is Mrs. Muggins, my housekeeper. Muggins, the ladies will be staying here for an indefinite time. I want you to take very good care of them."

"And do I need you to tell me that? They'll be as tenderly cared for as wee babes in their mothers' arms. Now, go wash up. I have lunch all ready."

"Presently. Right now I want you to take Cassie to the music room and show her the piano."

"The lass is musical? Come with me, Cassie, darlin'." Mrs. Muggins moved across the foyer in the direction of the French windows at the end of the hall. "We'll take a short cut across the terrace. Perhaps you'll play me a little tune."

Cassie trailed after the housekeeper, her gaze fixed in fascination on the mop of wild red curls affixed to Mrs. Muggins's round head. "What? Oh, sure I will."

"What about 'Galway Bay'?" Mrs. Muggins's head swiveled to look back at Andrew. "You rest up, now. I'll be back in a minute, Mr. Andrew."

Andrew's lips twisted ruefully. "I'm sure you will, Muggins."

"She's . . . a robot." Lily's whisper was dazed as she watched Mrs. Muggins's metal five-digit hand deftly open the French door. She was indisputably a stainless-steel robot, five feet in height, whose metal body and gleaming round shape still managed, in some impossible fashion, to look plump and motherly. The features on the round face were intricately carved to appear amazingly lifelike, and Lily would have sworn the round blue eyes flickered with expression. "Good Heavens, she's incredible."

"She's also a terrible nag," Andrew said in disgust.

"Only to those parties who need it," Mrs. Muggins retorted serenely as she rolled aside to allow Cassie to precede her. "As you do, Mr. Andrew." The robot glided after Cassie, closing the French door behind them.

"I don't believe it." Lily gazed blankly at the closed door. "I feel as if I've stepped onto the set of a *Star Wars* movie. I didn't think robots as sophisticated as that one existed yet."

"They didn't until my dear sister turned her hand to robotics." Andrew scowled. "I told Mariana she only created Mrs. Muggins to be the bane of my existence. The damn thing nags me to death."

"Then why don't you give her back to your sister?"

Andrew's scowl vanished, and he smiled sheepishly. "I guess I like her. Muggins kind of grows on you."

"Your sister must be a positive genius," Lily said. "Does she intend to patent the prototype?"

Andrew shook his head. "There are too many difficulties right now. It would revolutionize robotics and cast a glaring spotlight on the inventor. The Clanad can't afford the publicity."

"What a shame. It must be very frustrating for her."

"Mariana doesn't mind. She's too busy working on Mr. Muggins."

"I hesitate to ask what Mr. Muggins does."

"He's a gardener and a handyman." Andrew grinned. "Mariana's hoping to incorporate chauffeuring, but she tells me the judgment skills involved in driving are a nightmare."

"I'd like to meet her."

"You will. She's a curious imp. She won't be able to resist popping in to meet you and Cassie." Andrew's grin faded. "I've told everyone else to leave you alone for a few days to let you both become accustomed to your surroundings. I know it must seem very alien to you here."

"Well, I admit I don't run into motherly robots like Mrs. Muggins every day back home."

He nodded. "I've asked Quenby to select and send over a new wardrobe for you and Cassie. It should be delivered this afternoon."

"You're being very kind."

He shook his head. "I'm being very selfish. I want you to be happy here."

His gaze met hers, and Lily felt suddenly breathless. Sensuality. Where had it come from? Out of nowhere the sexual magnetism that had first drawn her to Andrew had come back in full strength. With an effort she pulled her gaze away. "You've certainly supplied the right ingredients."

"I tried. There's a darkroom, with several professional cameras, in one of the outbuildings."

"A darkroom?" Her eyes widened in surprise. "Are you a photographer too?"

He shook his head. "But when I had the house built I decided I'd provide for any eventuality. I knew you'd need one if you ever came here." He smiled. "You see, some sand castles aren't washed away, Lily. You're here in my house."

Lily felt her throat tighten with tears. Blast him, how was he able to do this to her? She knew the answer. The man was romantic, idealistic, and completely appealing. Dear heaven, she mustn't let him move her like that. "Well, I thank you for this particular sand castle. I promise I'll make good use of it."

"That's all I ask." He turned toward the door. "If you need anything, ask Muggins, and she'll either find it or phone and have it delivered."

"You're leaving?" Lily tried to hide the disappointment surging through her. "But this is your home. It's not right that I put you out."

"I want you to be comfortable," Andrew said softly. "You have adjustments to make, and I'm selfish enough to try to distract you if I'm in the same house."

She moistened her lips with her tongue. "It's a big house. We might never run into each other."

"But I'd see that we did." He smiled with frank sexuality. "And we might start a new roller-coaster ride before you were recovered from the old one. I can give you a day or so." He inclined his head. "With the greatest reluctance."

"Where will you stay?" Her voice sounded breathless even to her own ears.

"With Mariana. She has a place near the hospital, and I have some work that may need doing there."

"What kind of work?"

He shrugged. "Therapy." He opened the door. "Take care of yourself. I'll be in touch."

"Andrew," she called impulsively.

He stopped and looked at her inquiringly.

"I don't want . . ." She halted and started again. "I'm really quite adaptable. I'm not going to need a few days to settle in. Could you come back tomorrow and show me around the compound?"

A slow smile lit his face. "You mean it?"

She nodded, feeling suddenly light as air.

"You bet I will. Tomorrow at ten?"

"At ten."

The door closed behind him.

She shouldn't have called him back, she told herself. He had been willing to give her time, and she should have taken it and followed her usual course of caution and practicality. They were moving toward each other too quickly. She had been far too impulsive.

Still, a tiny smile curved her lips and her stride had a decided spring as she crossed the foyer to follow Mrs. Muggins and Cassie to the music room.

Gunner rose immediately to his feet as Andrew strode into the hospital waiting room. "I thought you'd be running over here the moment you were free," he said grimly. "I'm not letting you see him, Andrew."

"You can't stop me," Andrew said. "This is my territory, not yours. How is Kalom? Have they been able to reach him?"

Gunner shook his head. "They've been trying since the plane arrived here this morning. No response."

Andrew muttered a curse beneath his breath. "What the hell is the matter with him? I've never seen anyone so—" He stopped abruptly.

"So what?" Gunner asked. "Twisted? You forget I'm the one who locked him. I know what I saw there, and it was ugly as hell."

Andrew carefully guarded both his expression and his mind. Gunner evidently didn't realize Kalom's mind was more than ugly. The glimpse Andrew had taken had revealed a cesspool of rage and ferocity, of stored-up malice that was almost overpowering. "I can handle Kalom. I'm used to it."

Gunner snorted skeptically.

He knew as well as Andrew it was impossible to become accustomed to something that changed and evolved from moment to moment. The human mind reflected all facets of life, the beautiful as well as the ugly, but never remained the same.

"Who's working on him?" Andrew asked.

"The best. Debron and Braily. If they can't bring him out, no one can."

Andrew smiled and shook his head. "You know better. *I'm* the best, Gunner. I can go deeper."

"Stay out of it." Gunner's blue eyes held the chill of a Nordic winter. "He's not worth it. I won't have you risking yourself."

"What would you do? Lock me?"

"No, but I could kill Kalom."

Andrew stiffened. "You wouldn't do that."

"Try me." Gunner smiled with cold ferocity. "I have the option, and your life is a hell of a lot more valuable than his. Let the team do its work, and stay out of it. It shouldn't take more than a few days to break through."

Andrew studied him. "I think you're bluffing."

"Then call my bluff. Walk into that therapy room and you'll find a dead man."

Andrew hesitated. "I'll make a deal with you. I'll give them four days. After that, I'll go in."

"No deal."

"I'll go in," Andrew repeated softly. "And I'll stay, no matter what you do. Do you want me to be there when he dies, Gunner?"

Gunner met Andrew's hard stare and then turned away with barely restrained violence. "Dammit, you know he'd take you with him!" He pushed through the double doors leading to the therapy room. "But he's not going to get the chance. I'm going to tell Debron and Braily they have to break the lock or I'll skin them alive."

Eight

"It's incredible." Lily looked at the Chinese bridge arching over the rushing torrent of water, the rugged stones, the pines on the banks. "This park looks as if it's been transplanted from a national forest in Oregon, and yet your compound is set squarely in the middle of a desert. How could it be?"

"I told you we have some very talented people." Andrew opened the door of the car and helped her into the passenger seat. "They like to experiment. In fact, sometimes they go a little overboard. The council had to pass an ordinance demanding to see every plan before it was initiated, or the compound would be a terrible mishmash."

"I can't imagine that. It's perfectly beautiful." She glanced back at the park. "Different but definitely gorgeous."

Andrew smiled. "I'm glad you like us." He slammed the door and came around to the driver's side and got into the car.

"What's not to like?" The compound had obviously been built for ease of living, and its beauty was serene. The people she had met that day had the casual friendly attitude prevalent in small-town America. No, that wasn't quite true. Casual, perhaps, but there was no rocking-chair ambience about any of the compound's citizens. They seemed to possess a zestful, cheerful vitality that engendered an eager response in Lily.

Andrew started the car, gazing straight ahead as he asked in a low voice, "You don't think we're a bunch of freaks?"

"No." She thought about it. "Do you know it never occurred to me one time today that anyone I was meeting was in the least unusual? They were just nice, friendly people."

A delighted smile lit Andrew's face. "That's exactly what we are. We just have a different set of problems to face than most people."

Her eyes twinkled. "Kidnappings, foreign agents, viole—"

"That doesn't happen all the time," Andrew said, interrupting quickly. "Most of the time we live very peaceful lives here in Sedikhan."

"But you obviously don't always stay in Sedikhan," she said dryly. "For instance, what were you doing at Franklin University nine years ago? You said something about therapy."

Andrew nodded. "Henry needed help with a patient he couldn't reach, and sent out an SOS."

"Is Henry a member of the Clanad?"

"No, but he believes in what we're doing."

"I'm not sure I do."

Andrew stiffened and glanced sideways at her. "Why not?"

"This artificial insemination bothers me. I gather you don't tell the mother she'll have a telepathic surprise package a few years down the road. What if she doesn't want a headache like that?"

"We do tell them."

Lily's gaze flew to his face. "What?"

"They're told the donor has evidenced certain psychic abilities that might be inherited." He shrugged. "But most of them were skeptical."

"I wasn't told anything like that."

"I know." Andrew's hands tightened on the steering wheel. "I was afraid you'd reject me. I persuaded Henry not to give you the usual information. I know it was a dirty trick, but—" He stopped, looking at her in astonishment.

Lily was laughing.

"You're not angry?"

"I suppose I should be. The deck was obviously stacked against me from the beginning." She opened the car door. "Do you know what I would have done if Henry had told me? I would have laughed in his face, just like those other women. I *wanted* a baby. As long as Henry could assure me of mental stability, I wouldn't have cared if you'd claimed you could bend spoons at twenty paces." She got out of the car and glanced back. "By the way, can you?"

He shook his head. "Not my cup of tea." He got out of the driver's seat and shut the door. "Gunner probably could, but I don't think he'd waste his time."

Lily started up the curving path to the front door. "Did Henry have many rejections after he told the women about the possibilities?"

"None at all." He fell into step with her. "The possibilities intrigued them."

"Then why were you worried about my reaction?"

"Because you were walking a very fine emotional line, and it was too important to me to take the chance." He met her gaze. "*You* were too important."

Her chest felt suddenly tight, and it was hard to breathe. She was conscious of the sensitivity of her nipples as they pressed against the material of her bra; the scent of his woodsy cologne; the lean, warm strength of his body only inches away.

She hurriedly averted her gaze. "I don't see the point in encouraging all of you to spread these psychic powers anyway. The world's gotten along very well for centuries without them."

"But that wasn't the purpose at all." Andrew's tone was surprised. "We projected that the majority of the children born would only be latent telepaths, like Cassie."

"Then why?"

"The intelligence expansion could be inherited, and we didn't think it fair that we had a monopoly on it."

Lily stopped short. "Wait a minute. I think I've missed something."

He frowned. "I told you that those volunteers in Garvania had submitted to a mind-expansion chemical."

"From which they received telepathic talents."

"That was only the offshoot. I thought you realized that. The drug also opened approximately another thirty percent more of their brains for use."

"You . . . forgot to mention that," Lily said blankly.

"It doesn't make us superbrains. It only allows us to learn more."

"A colony of bloody geniuses," Lily said dazedly. "No wonder Said Ababa wants the Clanad back."

Andrew looked embarrassed. "It doesn't make us any different from anyone else."

"The hell it doesn't." She was thinking quickly. "Cassie. It was perfectly natural that Cassie turned out to be a child prodigy, wasn't it? Are the other children born from donors equally talented?"

"More or less."

She shook her head. "I feel like Alice in Wonderland."

"I don't know why you're so upset. I tell you, it's only a change in capacity. We're still very human. We make stupid blunders. We charge in where we shouldn't." He touched her cheek with his fingers with infinite gentleness. "We fall in love with women who refuse to love us back."

"Andrew . . ." She gazed at him helplessly. The additional information should have frightened and repelled her, but somehow it didn't. There was nothing frightening about Andrew, Gunner, or any of the people she had met since she had come to Sedikhan. Andrew was perhaps more vulnerable and human than anyone she had ever met. Just looking at that lean, gentle face she felt as if something inside her were breaking up, dissolving, melting. "I should go inside."

"In a minute." His finger moved down her cheek, and then her throat. "It seems as if I haven't touched you for a hundred years. Does it seem like that to you too?"

"Yes." His touch was gossamer-light, yet left a trail of tingling electricity in its wake. He placed one finger in the hollow of her throat, and she felt the betraying pulse leap in response.

"Do you remember that first night you came to me?" A flush mantled his cheekbones, and his eyes glittered fever-bright. "You were so tight, I was sure I was hurting you." He smiled as he felt the throb of her heart against the pad of his finger. "But then you held me tighter and tighter, until I thought you'd drive me out of my mind."

His touch, the erotic memories the words evoked, the sheer sensual *presence* of him were making her dizzy and weak. She could feel the muscles of her stomach clench as a tingling heat stabbed through her.

"I want it again. Now."

"No. Cassie . . ."

"Tonight, then. Are you in the master bedroom?"

She nodded dumbly.

"I'll come to you at eleven. Okay?"

Her lips were trembling as she tried to smile. "I think I'm being seduced again."

"I'm doing my damnedest." Andrew grinned with sudden boyishness. "A real bed, Lily. And time to lie in that bed with you and play and hold you all night if I want. Doesn't that sound great?"

A surge of maternal tenderness banished the last of her defenses. Sweet heaven, he was so dear. "Just great," she said shakily. "If Mrs. Muggins permits."

"Mrs. Muggins likes me to have what's good for me." He leaned forward and kissed her hard and sweet. "And you're very good for me. I'll send her to baby-sit Cassie." He opened the door behind her and gave her a little push into the foyer. "Eat dinner and then have a nice restful evening. You won't get much rest later."

"And will you be resting too?"

He hesitated. "I have to go over to the hospital for an hour or so."

"Therapy?" She frowned in concern. "Are you doing what you did with Cassie?"

He shook his head. "Nothing in depth. I'm just checking up on someone." His eyes twinkled. "But I promise I'll save plenty of energy."

He kissed her again, turned, and strolled down the path toward the car.

Lily gazed at her reflection in the bathroom mirror with dissatisfaction. Was she too pale? Perhaps she should put on a little more makeup. The emerald green of the satin robe went well with her chestnut hair, but it made her look surprisingly flamboyant. Perhaps she should change before Andrew got there. She still had fifteen minutes before he—

For Pete's sake, she was dithering like a nervous virgin, she thought in disgust. Those passionate encounters on the beach might just as well not have happened. She felt shy and scared, and yet so excited, butterflies were as active as Chinese acrobats in her stomach.

She would definitely change the robe, she decided as she turned and opened the door leading to the bedroom. The brown was more discreet, suited her personality, and she'd feel much more comfortable when—

Andrew was lying naked in the big double bed across the room, tanned and golden, his eyes gazing at her with glowing eagerness. A slow smile lit his face. "I couldn't wait."

She drew a deep breath, straightened her shoulders, and moved toward him. "You surprised me."

"I thought I'd present you with a *fait accompli.* I was afraid you'd change your mind." He met her gaze. "Have you?"

She moistened her lower lip with her tongue as she stopped before him. "No, but you mustn't take this to mean more than it does. Just because I want you doesn't mean—"

"Shhh." He knelt on the bed, the sheet falling away to reveal the hard length of his arousal. "Stop fighting me. We both know this means more than sex. You're taking another step toward me." His hands untied the belt at her waist and parted her robe. "Aren't you, love?"

He was right. No seduction had really been necessary this time. The decision to accept him in her bed had been her own, and meant more than she wanted to admit. "The lights . . ."

"Leave them on. I want to see you." His teeth

were nipping teasingly at her right breast. "That flashlight didn't cut it." His lips compressed, pulling gently at her nipple. "You don't mind, do you? You're so pretty."

Fire streaked through her, as his tongue teasingly soothed the nipple his teeth had nipped. "No." She gasped, not even aware of what she was saying. "Anything . . ."

He pulled her down on the bed, entering her with one deep stroke. She gasped and clutched desperately at his shoulders.

"My sentiments exactly," he muttered as he rotated within her. "Anything." His thrusts escalated to a wild, fierce rhythm. "And everything."

She heard something.

For an instant Lily stiffened, momentarily plummeted back to that terrifying moment at the beach house when Cassie had been taken.

No, Cassie was safe. This was Sedikhan, and Andrew was lying beside her, his heart still pounding hard beneath her ear. But she had definitely heard something, and Andrew must have heard it, too, for he was stiffening against her.

"My God, she's picking the lock."

"Who?" Lily whispered.

"I locked the door when I came in, but she's picking the damned lock!"

The door opened, and Mrs. Muggins glided into the room.

Lily couldn't help it. She started to laugh.

"It's not funny," Andrew said. "How the hell did she pick that lock?"

Mrs. Muggins was humming an Irish lullaby as she paused beside the bed, reached down and carefully drew up the sheet, and tucked it gently but firmly around both their shoulders. Then, breaking into the chorus of "When Irish Eyes are Smiling," she turned and rolled toward the door. "Sleep tight, now, darlin's."

The next instant she was gone.

Lily was laughing so hard, a stitch knifed through her left side. "Does she—" She had to stop for a moment. "Does she always tuck you in for the night?"

"Always," he said gloomily. "I'm going to kill Mariana."

"I think it's kind of sweet." Lily kissed his shoulder and then began to chuckle again. "But, yes, I definitely do have to meet your sister."

Mariana was dark, petite, and so charged with energy, it was like standing next to a lightning rod. She was also the frankest person Lily had ever run across.

Mariana breezed into the dining room the next morning when they were having breakfast, and immediately dominated the room.

"Hi, I'm Mariana." She kissed Andrew on the cheek, solemnly shook hands with Cassie, and winked at Lily. "No doubt my brother's been maligning me to you, but none of it's true. Trust me. May I have breakfast?" She plopped herself down in the chair across from Lily, appraising her openly. "Gosh, you're beautiful. What great cheekbones. Mrs. Muggins!"

"Right here." Mrs. Muggins instantly glided into the dining room from the kitchen area. "Ah, it's wonderful Miss Mariana."

Andrew snorted.

"Now, don't be disrespectful darlin'," Mrs. Muggins chided. "You know Miss Mariana is always right."

Lily started to laugh.

Mariana smiled blandly. "Of course you know that, Andrew. Why does she have to keep reminding you?"

"You should know. It's a little thing called programming."

"I'll just have toast and orange juice, Muggins," Mariana said.

"A very wise choice." Muggins turned and rolled out of the room.

"She made us have a full breakfast," Andrew glowered. "Protein, fruit, vegetables."

"But she realizes I know what's best for me. I incorporated excellent judgment into Muggins." Mariana leaned back in her chair and grinned at Lily. "Do you like her?"

"I love her." Lily chuckled. "She's a darling. She has a real personality."

Mariana nodded in satisfaction. "A combination Mother Macree and the quintessential electronic grandmother was what I had in mind."

Andrew rose to his feet. "I refuse to sit here and watch you pat yourself on the back for creating the bane of my life. Are you finished, Cassie? Let's go for a walk in the garden."

Cassie nodded and slipped from her chair. "Then

will you come to the music room? I finished the concerto. Mom heard it last night."

"Did she?" He smiled faintly as his gaze met Lily's. "Now, I wonder why she didn't remember to tell me?" He took Cassie's hand. "We'll go to the music room first. I can't wait."

Mariana watched them leave the room and then turned back to Lily. "He loves you, blast it. Do you know how lucky that makes you? Why the devil are you hesitating?"

Lily stiffened. "You're very blunt."

"I believe in going straight for the jugular." Mariana grinned. "Life is too short to complicate it by dithering. According to what Andrew tells me, you've had some rough breaks, but now it's time to clear the decks and start fresh. Andrew's been forced to wait too long for you as it is."

"I never asked him to wait."

"So what? He waited. And he'll probably keep on waiting. He's too tenderhearted to bulldoze the people he cares about." She wrinkled her nose. "He even puts up with my shenanigans."

A smile touched Lily's lips. "Mrs. Muggins?"

"Actually, I gave him Muggins for his own good. Andrew doesn't take proper care of himself." Mariana's smile faded. "And it's essential that he be in good physical condition for his work. I'm always afraid when he starts a therapy."

Fear surged through Lily. "There's danger?"

Mariana's lips twisted. "No more danger than wrestling with a homicidal maniac with no weapon to defend himself."

"What could happen to him?"

"You name it. The strain he undergoes is gigantic. Brain damage, coma, heart failure. Even the gentlest people have ferocious reactions when he's trying to undo a mental snarl. We seem to protect and nurture even the aberrations that are destroying us."

"Then why does he do it?"

"Because he cares." Mariana shook her head. "Because no one else can do it. Because he's Andrew."

"That's no reason to let him risk himself," Lily said fiercely. "Why don't you stop him? Why don't you tell him he's too valuable to be destroyed?"

"Why don't you? We've all tried, and gotten nowhere. Haven't you noticed? Andrew has a king-size sense of responsibility."

"Toward the entire human race? For Pete's sake, it's crazy to let him . . ." Lily trailed off as the tears rose to her eyes. She felt almost sick with fear and helplessness as she remembered how strained and ill Andrew had looked after he had finished helping Cassie. "There has to be some way to keep him safe."

"There is." Mariana met her gaze. "Stop thinking of your own problems and give him a reason for coming back when he goes under. You can't stop him from doing what he thinks is right, but you can hedge his gamble." She paused. "Don't you realize Andrew could straighten out your thinking any time he wanted if he treated you as he does a patient? But he won't go under and do that. He'll just wait and go through hell until you manage to see things clearly, because he respects your individual rights." She repeated softly, "And because he's Andrew."

Mrs. Muggins glided into the room and set a goblet of fresh-squeezed orange juice and a plate of toast on the table before Mariana. "There you are, Miss Mariana. Now, you eat a fine breakfast, so you can go back to work and make me lots of kinfolk."

Mariana stiffened with surprise. "Muggins, what—"

But Muggins had turned and rolled from the room.

"What's wrong?" Lily asked.

Mariana was gazing bemusedly at the doorway through which Muggins had vanished. "Nothing, probably. I just don't remember programming her with a desire for others of her kind." She shook her head as if to clear it. "But I must have done it. Right?" She picked up a triangle of toast and bit into it. "Now, where was I?"

Lily's eyes were twinkling. "Doing the bulldozing you said Andrew was too honorable to do."

"Oh, yes. Well, I've said enough to give you food for thought. I've never believed in overkill." She picked up her orange juice and sipped it. "Now tell me all about Cassie. I've never had a niece before."

Lily chuckled. "You march in here, accuse me of lallygagging, scare me half to death, and then rush on to something else. I'm beginning to believe there's a lot of you in Mrs. Muggins's programming."

"Maybe." Mariana grinned. "I tried to make her

as near human as possible, and no one can say
I'm not riddled with human idiosyncracies." She
gazed down into the orange juice in her goblet
before asking, with a touch of belligerence, "Do
you like me?"

"Yes." Lily found she liked Andrew's sister very
much indeed. She sensed something very appealing and vulnerable beneath the girl's dynamic,
eccentric surface. "I do like you."

Relief flickered on Mariana's face before she lowered her lids to hide it. "That's good," she said
offhandedly. "Not everybody does. Sometimes I'm
pretty hard to swallow."

Lily nodded. "Like a shot of straight vodka."

Mariana nodded. "You're honest. That's super.
I hate hypocrites." She took another swallow of
orange juice, set it down, and rose abruptly to her
feet. "I have to go."

Lily was startled. "Right now?"

"I have to get back to the laboratory to work on
Mr. Muggins, since we're through talking." She
frowned uncertainly. "Aren't we?"

She looked so like an anxious little girl that Lily
smothered a smile. "I believe you've covered the
major points."

Mariana moved toward the door. "I thought I
had. You just do what I've said, and everything
will work out." She left the room with neither a
backward glance nor a farewell.

The dining room seemed darker, as if a light
had gone out.

Mrs. Muggins rolled into the room and began to
clear Mariana's place, clucking reprovingly. "The

lass didn't even eat her toast. How can she expect to go on working the way she does, when she never eats? Oh, well, Miss Mariana always knows best." She whirled and glided toward the door. "Still, perhaps something should be done. . . ."

Lily shook her head in amusement as she placed her napkin on the table and stood up. Mariana might be in for a shock in the near future. Mrs. Muggins's programming seemed to be going awry, and off onto its own tangents.

Lily's smile vanished as she moved toward the door. She had a sudden desire to see Andrew, to touch him, to assure herself that he was well and safe. What Mariana had told her had frightened her badly. Andrew had been right when he had said that the night before had been a giant step forward in their relationship, but there was still a long way to go. She wasn't even sure she could maintain a permanent relationship, and she knew Andrew would accept nothing else.

Give him something to come back for, Mariana had said.

But that meant a commitment Lily wasn't ready to make.

Still, there was no hurry, she thought with relief. Andrew would be patient, and had told her he wasn't involved in any therapy at present. They would have time to work out their problems and come to a decision.

Yes, there was still plenty of time.

"The stars look closer here in Sedikhan." Lily

leaned back in the lawn chair, her gaze fixed dreamily on the glitter-sequined sky. "Why do you suppose that is?"

Andrew was sitting on a pillow on the flagstones of the terrace, beside her chair, and glanced up with a smile. "I could give you technical reasons, but I don't think you want them right now, do you?" He leaned his head comfortably against her knee. "You're more in the mood for fantasy."

"Nonsense. I'm a complete realist."

Yet she knew he was right. She was far too content sitting there with the gentle breeze touching her cheeks, teasing her with the scent of the flowering jasmine while she listened to the rippling sound of the fountain across the courtyard and to Cassie playing softly in the music room beyond the open French doors.

"I wonder on which star a rose could grow. Have you ever read *The Little Prince*?" Andrew asked.

"Yes, but I don't want to think of it right now. It's too sad."

"Only if you look at it from the viewpoint of a realist like one Lily Deslin."

"It's a sand-castle story."

"Yes." Andrew reached up and took her hand, threading his fingers through her own. "It makes me sad that you don't believe in sand castles."

"Sad? Why?"

"Because there's so much in life that you can't reach out and touch, so many things you lose if you don't keep them alive inside yourself." His lips brushed her palm. "I don't want you ever to lose anything. I want you to taste everything and know everything and feel everything. I want life to be so damned good to you that you'll wake up singing every morning."

Tenderness welled up in her, preventing her from speaking for a moment. "You'd soon regret it if I did. I can't carry a tune."

"You know what I mean."

"Yes." She wanted him to wake up singing too. She wanted his every hour to be golden, every wish granted, every foolish sand castle he built to last forever. "These last three days I admit I've come pretty close."

He held his hand to her cheek. "Me too." He paused. "Thank you."

"Thank you," she echoed softly. "It takes two."

"I want you to know what you've given me these last few days," he said quietly. "I used to think about how it would be to have you and Cassie here, but I didn't realize . . ." He stopped, and when he spoke again his voice was husky. "It's so *good.*" He fell silent, and it was several minutes before he continued. "I want you to know that if everything else were swept away I'd still be rich, because I'd have the memory of what we built together these last three days."

The faintest uneasiness rippled through her. "You're talking sand castles again. I don't like it."

"Sorry." He kissed her palm once more. "I just wanted you to know. Lie back and look up at the stars, and I'll tell you all about the constellations. I was fascinated by them as a boy, and memorized practically all the legends."

"Andrew." A troubled frown creased her brow as she looked down at him. She wished he'd look up again, so she could see his face. "Is something wrong?"

"What could be wrong?" He didn't look at her, and his voice was low. "It's just that I love you, Lily. I always have. I always will."

He was waiting for her to respond. She *wanted* to respond. For some reason she felt he needed those words of commitment from her that night. Dammit, why wouldn't the words come?

He was silent for a long moment, and then tilted his head back to gaze at the stars again. "That constellation is Leo, the lion." Andrew tilted back his head. "One of the stories I've read said that he angered Zeus by growling at him and . . ." The words drifted on as Andrew gave her the story from his childhood.

Gave. Andrew always gave to her, she thought in guilty anguish. He gave and gave. . . .

But that night he had asked for something in return, and she had failed him. She hadn't given him the words he needed to hear.

Next time she would do it, she promised herself. Next time she'd tell him she loved him.

Nine

As soon as Lily opened her eyes the next morning she realized Andrew was no longer beside her in the bed. His absence didn't alarm her. In the last few days she had learned he was a much earlier riser than she. He must be in the bathroom, she thought lazily, or out on the balcony. He loved to watch the sun rise over the desert.

Lily reached over and with a caressing hand touched the indentation on the pillow where his head had lain. It was strange how many little things signaled this major upheaval in her life. The sight of the change from Andrew's pockets on top of the bureau, the sound of a shower running in the next room, Andrew's quick footsteps on the stairs or in the hall. Such little, unimportant things to engender such flowering feelings of warmth and security.

The phone rang on the table beside the bed,

and she reached over to pick up the receiver. "Hello."

"Lily." It was Quenby's voice. "Listen carefully. I'm sending a car for you. Be out in front of the house in ten minutes."

Lily sat up in bed. "Why? I'll have to ask Andrew what plans—" She broke off as the crackling urgency of Quenby's tone sank in. "What's wrong?"

"Andrew."

Blind panic seized Lily. Andrew wasn't in the bathroom or out on the balcony. Andrew wasn't in the house at all. Her hand tightened on the receiver. "What's happened to him?"

"I don't know." Quenby drew a shaky breath. "As God is my witness, I don't know. He's at the hospital, and it's not going well. Gunner was planning on being there this morning before Andrew arrived, but Andrew showed up in the therapy room three hours ago. He knew Gunner would try to stop him, and immediately started treating Kalom." She paused. "The doctors noticed something wrong almost at once. Andrew went into convul—"

"Save the rest of it," Lily cut in as she swung her feet to the floor. "I have to get dressed and get downstairs. Will you be at the hospital when I get there?"

"I'm in the waiting room with Mariana."

"She's there too?" Lily closed her eyes. Of course Mariana was at the hospital. They always called the next of kin in life-or-death emergencies. Dear God, was Andrew dying? She should have known something would happen to explode the dream.

But it shouldn't have happened to Andrew. Perhaps she didn't deserve her happiness with him after the mistakes she had made, but Andrew shouldn't be punished. "I'll be right there."

She put down the receiver, jumped out of bed, and ran to the bathroom.

"Is he still alive?" Lily demanded as soon as she strode into the waiting room. "For God's sake, what happened to him?"

"Kalom," Quenby said simply. "Gunner thinks Kalom is trying to die and wants to take Andrew with him."

"I don't understand. Can that happen?"

Mariana turned away from the window. "They're joined telepathically. It can happen."

"But if Andrew's trying to help him, why would Kalom want to kill him?"

"Who knows? He's twisted," Quenby said. "Gunner says his mind's like a desert where nothing can grow but malice, and the malice is so bitter, he chokes on it. He *wants* to die."

"Then let him die," Lily said fiercely.

"But he won't let Andrew go," Mariana said. "Or Andrew won't let him go, we don't know which." Her teeth pressed hard into her lower lip. "Andrew's in a coma."

Lily felt as if an iron hand were crushing her heart, stopping her blood from flowing. "Gunner," she said desperately. "Can't Gunner help?"

Quenby shook her head. "Andrew's too deep." She gazed squarely at Lily. "The vital signs of both men are weakening. They can't last much longer unless something changes."

"You're telling me there's no chance?" Lily whispered. "I won't believe that. Andrew is so strong. He won't give up. I won't let him give up."

"You can't help him," Mariana said dully as she turned away to look out the window again. "None of us can help him now. We've always been terrified this would happen to Andrew someday."

They were giving up. She couldn't believe it. Mariana and Quenby were two of the strongest women she had ever met. Didn't they realize something had to be done? "The hell I can't. Where is this therapy room?"

Quenby gestured to the double doors across the room. "Gunner's doing all he can, Lily. You're not even a telepath. You can't expect to—"

"So I'm not some kind of mind wizard. You're all relying too much on this telepathy business. I can expect to do anything I damn well set out to do. I won't let him go just because you say it's telepathically impossible. To *hell* with telepathy." Lily whirled on her heel and strode in the direction Quenby had indicated. "Do you think I'd let that slime bag take Andrew away from me?"

She pushed through the heavy double doors and was immediately assaulted by the smell of antiseptic. Kalom occupied a hospital bed on the far side of the room, but Lily hardly glanced at him. Her entire attention was focused on Andrew's still form, lying in the bed closest to the door.

She gave a low cry as she caught sight of his face. "Dear heaven."

Pain. His features were contorted in the same terrible grimace she'd seen on the faces of Kalom and Baharas the day Andrew and Gunner had rescued Cassie.

"You shouldn't be here." Gunner moved forward from the corner of the room, where he'd been standing. "You can't help him, Lily."

"That's what Quenby said." Lily's eyes glittered with unshed tears. "He's hurting, isn't he? That bastard is hurting him."

"Yes."

"And you can't stop it?"

Gunner shook his head.

"All this psychic nonsense, all these superbrains running around the compound," Lily said in wonder. "And none of you can help Andrew?"

"Lily—"

She made a motion with her hand. "Oh, I know what you're going to say. Andrew told me that the Clanad's powers didn't make any difference. That in the end it was their humanity that mattered." She moved toward Andrew's bed. "Well, I don't know anything about this telepathic business, but I won't let Andrew go on hurting without trying to comfort him."

She lay down on the bed beside Andrew, achingly conscious of how stiff he was, the muscles rigid and unyielding against her. She put her arms around him and laid her cheek in the hollow of his shoulder. "Andrew." She closed her eyes, her voice no louder than a breath. "I need you so. Don't leave me."

Andrew didn't stir.

"Do you remember how you told me I had to forgive myself for failing? Well, that's what you have to do too. If you can't help him, accept it and forgive yourself." Her fingers started to stroke the fair hair at his left temple. "I'll make a deal with you. I'll forgive myself if you'll do the same for yourself. Okay?"

Bargains. Was it Andrew with whom she was trying to bargain or was it God? "You might as well come back, because I'm not going to let you die. I'm not letting you go anywhere without me ever again. Do you hear me?"

No answer.

She could feel Gunner's sympathetic gaze on her, but she ignored it. She knew he thought her efforts were useless, that she was building a sand castle that would be swept away by forces beyond her control.

"I'm going to stay right here," she whispered to Andrew. "And soon you're going to open your eyes and smile at me. I'm going to stay right here and hold you and wait for you to come back." She would not cry. She had to concentrate on sending all the love and confidence she had to Andrew. She had no time to weep, when all her strength had to be channeled toward Andrew. "Please stop hurting, love. I can't bear it."

Andrew didn't answer.

But he *would* respond. She mustn't give up hope. Andrew wouldn't leave her to loneliness again. She had only to be patient and wait for him. She nestled closer, sharing her warmth, sharing her love. "Come back. . . ."

• • • •

But it was not until over six hours later that Andrew's condition underwent a change.

"Kalom's dead, Lily!" Gunner's voice cracked, lash-sharp, as he strode across the room, his gaze narrowed on Andrew's face. "Just now. Get up. I have to check Andrew."

Lily sat bolt upright, her eyes widening in horror. "Dead? But you said that could mean Andrew—"

"Yes, dammit." Gunner's voice gentled. "I'm sorry, Lily, but a survival is very rare in cases—"

Andrew opened his eyes!

"Thank God," Gunner said thickly.

"Andrew," Lily whispered.

"I failed." Tears glittered in Andrew's eyes. "I couldn't keep him. I tried to tell him that everything could be different, but he wouldn't listen. . . ."

Joy illuminated Lily's face. "But you're alive. He didn't take you."

"I failed." Andrew's eyes closed wearily. "So much pain and rage. He needed me, and I failed him."

"It doesn't matter," Lily said fiercely. "For heaven's sake, he wanted to kill you. He doesn't matter."

"He matters. Everyone matters. That's what life is all about. . . ." His voice trailed off as his breathing deepened in the rhythm of sleep.

Lily's alarmed glance flew to Gunner's face.

"It's all right. It's only exhaustion." He was smiling reassuringly. "He'll probably sleep around the clock."

"He's safe?" she asked. She couldn't believe it.

Gunner nodded. "He's going to be fine."

"Then I want him home, where I can take care

of him. Will you arrange for an ambulance?" She glanced at Kalom's still body lying on the bed across the room, and a shudder ran through her. How could Andrew feel anything but hatred for the man who had tried to kill him? "I don't like it here."

Gunner helped her from the bed. "That's not a bad idea. Andrew's not accustomed to failing, and it isn't going to be easy for him to face the fact that he couldn't help Kalom."

"No one else would have tried. I don't know why he did."

"Yes, you do," Gunner said quietly. "He told you. Everyone matters to Andrew."

She nodded, and swallowed to ease the tightness in her throat as she glanced back at Andrew's face. Yes, she knew why Andrew had been compelled to try to help Kalom even if it meant endangering his own life. "I'll go tell Quenby and Mariana he's all right." She turned to leave, and then abruptly swung back to face him. "I *did* help him, didn't I?"

A warm smile lit Gunner's face. "You bet. Andrew's vital signs began to steady from the moment you lay down beside him. It surprised the hell out of me."

"You shouldn't have been surprised. I just used a universal panacea that's been around a good deal longer than anything the Clanad's come up with." She grinned as she opened the door. "Andrew and I made a deal."

• • •

Gunner was right. Andrew slept around the clock, woke for a few minutes, and then immediately fell asleep again.

"He's sad again, isn't he?" Cassie whispered, edging close to the bed to gaze down at him.

"Yes, something happened to make him very sad, love." Lily took Cassie's hand and held it tightly as waves of emotion spiraled through her. He looked more like a weary little boy than the virile man she knew so well, yet the boy was every bit as lovable as the man. "But Andrew's going to be fine. We're going to make sure he is, aren't we?"

Cassie nodded.

"And I know how," Lily said as the idea suddenly occurred to her. "Will you help me?"

"If I can."

"Oh, you can." Lily propelled her from the bedroom and then down the stairs. "What I have in mind is definitely in your area of expertise. Call Mrs. Muggins and tell her we'll need a car to take a drive into the desert."

"The desert?"

"And we'll need some tools." Lily frowned in concentration. "Hurry, love. We may not have much time before he wakes up again."

Cassie ran down the hall in search of Mrs. Muggins while Lily crossed to the telephone and picked up the receiver to call Mariana, Quenby, and Gunner.

Andrew was standing on the balcony, framed against the scarlet-and-purple skies of the sunset, when Lily walked into the room. He immediately turned around when he heard the door open, and smiled at her. "I'm afraid I haven't been too sociable lately," he said lightly as he held out his hand to her. "Gunner was just here, and said I've been out of it for nearly two days."

"You needed the rest." She came onto the balcony and took the hand he held out, her gaze anxiously searching his face. His color was good, the lines of exhaustion gone, she noted with relief, but he appeared thinner. "Have you lost weight?"

He shrugged. "I usually lose a few pounds after one of these sessions. I'll gain it back in a few days."

"See that you do. No wonder Mariana gave you Muggins. You don't take care of yourself."

"That was no reason to inflict the 'irresistible force' on my hapless head." He lifted her hand to his lips and pressed a kiss on the palm. "But I promise I'll eat every one of my vegetables at your command. Gunner tells me I owe you."

"Gunner's right," she said crisply. "And I intend to collect."

Surprise crossed his face. "With what kind of exchange?"

"Exchange is the right term. This is a two-way street, you know. I don't want any more of this nonsense with creeps like Kalom. It's bad enough that you risk your life with people who have essential worth. I won't have you—" She found her voice was shaking, and was forced to stop to steady it. "I'd like to say, 'Don't ever do anything like that again,' but I won't. I know your work is too important to stop. All I ask is that you not take unnecessary risks. Okay?"

"Okay." His long fingers traced the line of her cheekbone with infinite tenderness. "But you're wrong about not trying to save people like Kalom, Lily. They need help more than the others." His expression became wistful. "Can't you see how tragic they are? We all start out the same, clean and shining and new, but then ugly things twist and corrode some people until all that wonderful shining is buried."

She gazed at him in helpless exasperation. She was back at square one. "And you have to be the one to scrape off the corrosion."

He frowned. "I hoped you'd understand."

"Oh, I understand. I wish I didn't. I wish I could say, 'Sorry, Andrew, this is going to be too much of a hassle. I think I'll bow out.' " She shook her head. "But it doesn't work that way."

He stiffened warily. "Are you trying to tell me something?"

"I'm trying to tell you that I was probably better off with a five-star louse like Tait than with a man who's single-handedly trying to save the whole bloody world." She blinked hard to keep the tears from falling. "You're not practical or sensible, and you believe in dreams and people that shine inside and—"

"People do shine," Andrew interrupted. "You shine, Lily. Years ago, when I first saw you, I thought you shone like silver, but now it's more like burnished copper. Warm and deep and rich with—"

"See? You don't even think like anyone else. You'd let me hurt you. You'd let *anyone* hurt you if you thought it would help that person." She took a step back. "Well, no one will do it,' she said fiercely. "I won't let that happen. Do you hear me? You're not going to be a damn martyr. You're going to live a long, long life, and you're going to be happy. You're going to be so damn happy— Stop laughing. I mean it."

"I know." He smiled at her, his eyes still sparkling with amusement. "That's why I'm laughing. Pure, unadulterated relief. You had me scared for a minute, but, if I'm not mistaken, I do believe you're trying to make a declaration."

"A declaration? You want a declaration?" She took his hand and pulled him through the French doors leading to the bedroom, and then toward the door to the hall. "I'll show you a declaration."

Ten

"May I ask where we're going?" Andrew asked as she ushered him swiftly down the steps. "Merely as a point of curiosity, you understand. I'm quite willing to follow you to the ends of the earth."

"The terrace," Lily said tersely.

"And what awaits us on the terrace? A candlelight supper with a gypsy violinist? Or perhaps a single red rose lying beside my plate?"

"No." She pulled him with her toward the terrace.

"What a disappointment. I was hoping for a romantic gesture at last from my pragmatic Lily."

"You're taking this all wrong. I'm very serious."

He stopped her with a hand on her arm as she reached for the knob of the French door. She glanced up to meet his gaze and caught her breath. His eyes were glowing with a radiant joy. "I have to joke. I don't know what else to do. This means too much to me, and I've wanted for it too long. I feel like soaring up to the sky like a bird or banging out Chopsticks on Cassie's piano or—"

"I think you've made yourself clear." She smiled tremulously as she threw open the door. "Behold the declaration."

On a large table beside the pool stood a splendid sand castle, whose intricately carved turrets and battlements towered six feet into the air. The scarlet rays of the setting sun bathed the structure in a rosy glow, capturing glimmers of gold in the sand that turned it into a fantasy castle straight from the pages of a child's fairy tale.

Andrew stood very still in the doorway, staring at it silently.

"Do you like it?" Lily pulled him out on the terrace. "I didn't do it all my myself. Quenby, Mariana, Gunner, and Cassie helped. And Mrs. Muggins did those tiny windows in the tower. You'd be amazed how dexterous her metal fingers can be." Lily released his hand and turned to face him. "But the idea was mine."

He was still silent.

"Well, say something," she said with a nervous laugh. "I'm beginning to feel foolish. I'm not used to making grandiose gestures like this."

"Vive la déclaration." His gaze finally shifted from the sand castle to her face. "Now, can you put it into words?"

"Pushy. You're always so pushy." Her lids lowered to veil her eyes. "It's not easy."

"Neither was building that sand castle."

"You're right. It was damn frustrating, knowing all that effort was going to be history in an hour or a day."

"But you did it."

"I wanted to show you . . ." She gazed directly into his eyes. "I won't ever believe entirely, as you do, but I can agree on fundamentals. I'll trust your integrity until the day I die, and I believe that there are some things that can't be destroyed by time or circumstances. Is that enough?"

"Enough," he said softly. "It's the fundamentals that count. I never expected you to be a carbon copy of me, to believe all I believe."

She nodded and took a deep breath. "Okay. Now for the big plunge." She paused, then said in a rush, "And I believe one of those things that can't be destroyed is love. And I do love you and inend to love you through hell and high water and—"

"Easy." He took a step closer and drew her into his arms. "It doesn't all have to come at once."

"Yes, it does. I'm on a roll. You should have made me tell you this before, instead of being so damn patient. I was so scared I wouldn't get the chance, when I saw you lying in that hospital bed." She rested her head on his shoulder. He felt so good, so male, so . . . Andrew. "You're an extraordinary human being, and I respect and admire you." Her arms slipped around his neck. "But most of all I love you. You can be anything you want to be, do anything you want to do, and that fact will never change. You can build sand castles to the sky and risk your life with scum like Kalom and I'll still be here. I won't change and I won't go away."

"That's quite a roll," he said thickly. "Am I allowed to say I reciprocate your feelings?"

"No, because you already told me in that idioti-
cally generous way you have." Her arms tightened
around him. "You just gave it to me and didn't
ask anything in return. Something's really got to
be done about you."

"Marriage?"

She stiffened. "I never thought—"

He pushed her back to look down into her face.
"Since we have an eight-year-old child, I believe
it's time we did think about it." His eyes were
twinkling. "Think how much power you'd have
over me if you had me all trussed up in the mari-
tal noose."

She shook her head. "You'll still do exactly what
you want to do."

"And I want to marry Lily Deslin. Now, since you
claim your affections won't change, can you think
of an argument against it?"

She shook her head as heady joy exploded within
her. "Not even one."

He kissed her gently. "Tomorrow?"

She shook her head. "You said your parents will
be back from Marasef next week. I want them to
meet me first." A shadow temporarily banished
the smile from her face. "I wish my mother could
have met you, Andrew. She always wanted me to
have a marriage as good as her own. Do you suppose she knows?"

His hands framed her face, and he looked down
at her gravely. "I believe people don't die as long
as their memory lives on."

"That's not enough. I want to believe she knows
and is happy for me. Perhaps I do believe it." Her

eyes glimmered with tears as she gazed up at him. "Another sand castle. Maybe I'm coming closer to your way of thinking than I first imagined."

"Perhaps you are." He kissed her with glowing sweetness and then let her go. "And now I want to examine this magnificent sand castle you've built for me."

Her eyes widened as she put out a hand to stop him. "You can do that later. Why don't we go get Cassie from her room? I promised we'd have a really festive dinner."

Andrew looked at her in surprise. "It will only take a minute."

"But you know how testy Muggins is when you're late to dinner. She'll nag you to—" She stopped as she met his quizzical glance, and heaved a resigned sigh. "All right, you might as well know now as later. Go look at it."

Andrew turned and crossed the few yards separating them from the sand castle on the table. "Now, what could you have done to make you look so guilty?" he muttered as he bent down and examined the wall surrounding the castle. "It's a great castle, a fantastic castle. I couldn't have done better myself. Why are you—" He reached out and touched the wall surrounding the sand castle with a probing index finger.

He stiffened in surprise.

He touched the wall again.

Then he threw back his head and started to laugh.

"I just couldn't bear it," Lily said quickly. "This sand castle was going to *mean* something. It's all very well to believe in things that we can't see, but won't it be nice to have something substantial to look at and remind us of tonight and—"

"Lily, stop apologizing." Andrew wiped his eyes with the back of his hand. "What the devil did you use?"

"Quick-drying cement. I mixed it with the sand and water. We had to work very fast."

"I just bet you did."

"You're not angry?" she whispered. "I told you I'm not like you. I need to have some of my dreams founded in cement, where I can touch them. You said it was only the fundamentals that mattered, and I promise you those will stand alone, Andrew."

He shook his head in amusement as he turned to look at the sand castle again. "Why should I be angry? I think it will be great to have a castle around the house. I'd like to put it in my pocket and take it with me everywhere."

"Really?" She knew Andrew didn't need to carry his sand castles with him, but he understood that she did. He always understood what was important and tried to give it to her. "You'd find that difficult to do." She smiled brilliantly, her face illuminated with love. "And besides, it's not necessary. No matter what road we travel, we'll always know it's here waiting for us."

His joyous smile mirrored her own. "Yes," he said softly. "We'll always know what we have waiting for us."

THE EDITOR'S CORNER

There is never a dull moment in our LOVESWEPT offices where we're forever discussing new ideas for the line. So, fair warning, get ready for the fruits of two of our brainstorms . . . which, of course, we hope you will love.

First, expect a fabulous *visual* surprise next month. We are going to reflect the brilliance of our LOVESWEPT author's romances by adding *shimmer* to our covers. Our gorgeous new look features metallic ink frames around our cover illustrations. We've also had a calligrapher devote his talent to reworking the LOVESWEPT lettering into a lacy script and it will be embossed in white on the top metallic border of the books. Each month has a color of its own. (Look for gleaming blue next month . . . for glimmering rosy red the following month.) So what will set apart the books in a given month? Well, the author's name, the book's title, and a tiny decorative border around the art panel will have its own special color. Just beautiful. We've worked long and hard on our new look, and we're popping with prideful enthusiasm for it. Special thanks go to our creative and tireless art director, Marva Martin.

Around here we believe that resting on laurels must be boring (could it also be painful?). And, like most women, all of us LOVESWEPT ladies, authors and editors, are out to prove something as time goes by—namely, *the older we get . . . the better we get . . . in every way!*

Our exciting news has taken so much space that I'm afraid I can give only brief descriptions of the wonderful romances we have coming your way next month. However, I'm sure that just the names of the authors will whet your appetite for the terrific love stories we have in our bright new packages.

Delightful Kay Hooper has come up with a real treat—not just one, but many—the first of which you'll get to sample next month. Kay is writing a number of LOVE-SWEPTs that are based on fairy tales . . . but bringing

(continued)

their themes completely (and excitingly!) up to date. Next month, *Once Upon a Time* ... **GOLDEN THREADS**, LOVESWEPT #348, tells the love story of Lara Mason who, like Rapunzel, was isolated in a lonely, alien life ... until Devon Shane came along to help her solve the problems that had driven her into hiding. An absolutely unforgettable romance!

In a book that's as much snappy fun as its title, Doris Parmett gives us **SASSY**, LOVESWEPT #349. Supermodel Sassy Shaw thought she was headed for a peaceful vacation in Nevada, but rancher Luke Cassidy had other plans for his gorgeous guest. This is a real sizzler ... with lots of guffaws thrown in. We think you'll love it.

The thrilling conclusion of The Cherokee Trilogy arrives from Deborah Smith next month with **KAT'S TALE**, LOVESWEPT #350. Kat Gallatin, whom you've met briefly in the first two of the Cherokee books, is unorthodox ... to say the least. She's also adorable and heartwarming, a real heroine. That's what Nathan Chatham thinks, too, as he gets involved with the wildcat he wants to see turn kitten in his arms. A fabulous conclusion to this wonderful trio of books—a must read!

Tami Hoag tugs at your heart in **STRAIGHT FROM THE HEART**, LOVESWEPT #351. Jace Cooper, an injured baseball star, was back in town, and Rebecca Bradshaw was desperate to avoid him—an impossibility since she was assigned to be his physical therapist. In this sizzler Rebecca and Jace have to work out the problems of a wild past full of misunderstanding. **STRAIGHT FROM THE HEART** is a sensual and emotional delight from talented Tami.

Patt Bucheister gives us another real charmer in **ELUSIVE GYPSY**, LOVESWEPT #352. Rachel Hyatt is a Justice of the Peace who married Thorn Canon's aunt to some stranger ... and he's furious when he first encounters her. But not for long. She makes his blood boil (not his temper) and thoroughly enchants him with her

(continued)

off-beat way of looking at the world. Don't miss this marvelous love story!

THE WITCHING TIME, LOVESWEPT #353, by Fayrene Preston is delicious, a true dessert of a romance, so we saved it for the end of LOVESWEPT's September feast. Something strange was going on in Hilary, Virginia. Noah Braxton felt it the second he arrived in town. He knew it when he encountered a golden-haired, blue-eyed witch named Rhiannon York who cast a spell on him. With his quaint aunts, Rhiannon's extraordinary cat, and a mysterious secret in town, Noah finds his romance with the incredible Rhiannon gets unbelievably, but delightfully, complex. A true confection of a romance that you can relish, knowing it doesn't have a single calorie in it to add to your waistline.

We hope you will enjoy our present to you of our new look next month. We want you to be proud of being seen reading a LOVESWEPT in public, and we think you will be with these beautifully packaged romances. Our goal was to give you prettier and more discreet covers with a touch of elegance. Let us know if you think we succeeded.

With every good wish,

Carolyn Nichols

Carolyn Nichols
Editor
LOVESWEPT
Bantam Books
666 Fifth Avenue
New York, NY 10103

BANTAM NEVER SOUNDED SO GOOD
NEW SUBLIMINAL SELF-HELP TAPES
FROM BANTAM AUDIO PUBLISHING
Invest in the powers of your mind.

Years of extensive research and personal experience have proved that it is possible to release powers hidden in the subconscious through the rise of subliminal suggestion. Now the Bantam Audio Self-Help series, produced by Audio Activation, combines sophisticated psychological techniques of behavior modification with subliminal stimulation that will help you get what you want out of life.

☐ 45106	**GET A GOOD NIGHT'S SLEEP . . .** **EVERY NIGHT: FEMALE**	$7.95
☐ 45107	**GET A GOOD NIGHT'S SLEEP . . .** **EVERY NIGHT: MALE**	$7.95
☐ 45041	**STRESS-FREE FOREVER: FEMALE**	$8.95
☐ 45042	**STRESS-FREE FOREVER: MALE**	$8.95
☐ 45081	**YOU'RE IRRESISTIBLE!: FEMALE**	$7.95
☐ 45082	**YOU'RE IRRESISTIBLE!: MALE**	$7.95
☐ 45004	**SLIM FOREVER: FOR WOMEN**	$8.95
☐ 45005	**SLIM FOREVER: FOR MEN**	$8.95
☐ 45022	**POSITIVELY CHANGE YOUR LIFE: FOR WOMEN**	$7.95
☐ 45023	**POSITIVELY CHANGE YOUR LIFE: FOR MEN**	$7.95
☐ 45035	**STOP SMOKING FOREVER: FOR WOMEN**	$7.95
☐ 45036	**STOP SMOKING FOREVER: FOR MEN**	$7.95
☐ 45094	**IMPROVE YOUR CONCENTRATION: WOMEN**	$7.95
☐ 45095	**IMPROVE YOUR CONCENTRATION: MEN**	$7.95
☐ 45112	**AWAKEN YOUR SENSUALITY: FEMALE**	$7.95
☐ 45113	**AWKAEN YOUR SENSUALITY: MALE**	$7.95
☐ 45130	**DEVELOP INTUITION: WOMEN**	$7.95
☐ 45131	**DEVELOP INTUITION: MEN**	$7.95
☐ 45016	**PLAY TO WIN: WOMEN**	$7.95
☐ 45017	**PLAY TO WIN: MEN**	$7.95
☐ 45010	**WEALTH, COME TO YOU: FEMALE**	$7.95
☐ 45011	**WEALTH, COME TO YOU: MALE**	$7.95

Look for them at your local bookstore, or use this handy page to order.

- -

Bantam Books, Dept. BAP4, 414 East Golf Road, Des Plaines, IL 60016

Please send me _____ copies of the tapes I have checked. I am enclosing $_____ (please add $2.00 to cover postage and handling). Send check or money order—no cash or C.O.D.s please.

Mr/Ms _____

Address_____

City/State _____ Zip _____

BAP4—6/89

Please allow four to six weeks for delivery. This offer expires 12/89. Prices and availability subject to change without notice.